PLAIN JANE
IN THE
SPOTLIGHT

PLAIN JANE IN THE SPOTLIGHT

BY

LUCY GORDON

First published in Great Britain 2012
by Mills & Boon, an imprint of Harlequin (UK) Limited.
Large Print edition 2012
Harlequin (UK) Limited, Eton House,
18-24 Paradise Road, Richmond, Surrey TW9 1SR

ISBN: 978 0 263 22618 8

Harlequin (UK) policy is to use papers that are natural,
renewable and recyclable products and made from
wood grown in sustainable forests. The logging and
manufacturing process conform to the legal environmental
regulations of the country of origin.

Printed and bound in Great Britain
by CPI Antony Rowe, Chippenham, Wiltshire

CHAPTER ONE

'FOR pity's sake, Travis, why do you never listen? You've been warned a dozen times. *Stay out of sleazy nightclubs.*'

Denzil Raines, boss of the Sandora Studio in Los Angeles, snapped out the command and tried to control his temper. It was hard because Travis would try anyone's patience.

The studio produced several money-making television series, but none of them raked in the wealth as fast and gloriously as *The Man From Heaven*, starring Travis Falcon, and protecting that investment was a major operation.

The young man enduring the lecture seemed to sum up the whole of the investment in himself. Travis's body was lean and vigorous, his face was handsome, his air charming, his smile devastating. It spoke of eagerness to enjoy life to the full. Late nights, curiosity for new experiences, untiring energy for a vast range of pleasurable activities.

They were all there in the quirk of his mouth, the gleam in his eye, and they caused much hair tearing among those who needed to keep him in check.

Denzil reflected that he'd picked the right word. Sleazy. That was it. Sleazy nightclubs, sleazy pleasures, sleazy Travis. But he knew it was precisely the hint of a 'bad boy' lurking in the shadows that hit the magic spot with the public. And it would go on doing so as long as it stayed in the safety of the shadows. If it was allowed to escape… Denzil groaned.

Travis was standing by the window, looking out over the view of Los Angeles. Clearly visible in the distance was the huge gleaming sign, HOLLYWOOD, that for ninety years had symbolised the city where glamour, entertainment and money united in brilliant supremacy. His gaze was fixed on the sign, as though to remind himself of the achievements he was fighting to keep. He stood, bathed in sunlight, apparently nonchalant, but actually alive to every threatening nuance.

'I didn't know it was sleazy,' he said with a shrug. 'My friend chose it for his stag night.'

'Stag night?' Denzil echoed in outrage. 'Then you might have guessed there'd be half-naked dolly birds prancing around. What else are stag nights for? You should have got out of the place instead of…*this*!'

He held out a newspaper, jamming his finger down on a picture of a man and a girl clinging to each other. He was sitting down, shirt ripped open, the half-naked girl on his lap, her arms about his neck, kissing him madly, which he showed every sign of enjoying.

'You had to lay yourself out for those girls,' Denzil groaned.

'I didn't lay myself out,' Travis protested. 'I was having a quiet drink when this lady…well…'

'Quiet? Hah! When did you last do anything quietly? And she was no lady. She'd been hired for the night to "entertain" the male guests. She entertained you all right.'

'I didn't ask her to sit on my lap.'

'You didn't push her off, either.'

'No, that would have been rude. I was just trying to be polite.'

'Oh, it was politeness that made you put your arms about her waist, draw her close, nuzzle her—'

'I'm only human,' Travis protested. 'When a

half-naked girl drapes herself over a guy he's expected to show some appreciation.'

'You did that all right,' Denzil snapped. 'She's not the only one who's half-naked. Look at your shirt, open to the waist, so that she can dance her fingers over your bare chest. Did she pull it open? Did *you*? Or did you arrive like that, hoping something would happen?'

Travis groaned. 'Can we just leave this? I didn't know the press was there, OK?'

'The press is always there where you're concerned,' Denzil growled. 'You should know that by now. Ever since the show became a hit they've been watching you, trying to find out something that makes people's hair stand on end. And, let's face it, there are plenty of those!'

'I refuse to answer on the grounds that it may incriminate me,' Travis said with a touch of wry humour.

'Very wise. They just want to catch you out with something really damaging. It wouldn't be such a problem if you were playing a different character, but this one is full of danger.'

The TV series, *The Man From Heaven*, was the talk of the entertainment world. Superficially, it seemed a conventional hospital drama, centred around the young, handsome Dr Brad Harrison, played by Travis Falcon. But beneath it was another tale. The doctor lived a life of strict virtue that was wildly at odds with his flamboyant sexual presence, and there was just a hint that he wasn't a mortal man at all, but a spirit from another dimension.

It was the intriguing contrast between Dr Harrison's austere life and the sexual indulgence open to a man of his attractions that had sent the show to the top of all the popularity charts. The producers were determined to keep it there, if only they could rein in Travis's more lurid off-screen activities.

'Folk out there like nothing better than to discover "the heavenly being" acting on his lowest human instincts,' Denzil pointed out now.

'But I'm not a heavenly being,' Travis said firmly.

'You don't have to tell me that,' Denzil snapped. 'Look, the public's crazy about you, the money's pouring in. The next series is being planned. But that could all change if you step too much out of character in private. Look, I'm not unreasonable.

Of course you want female company. Just not *that* sort.'

Travis studied the picture again and sighed. 'I know. I was careless. I'll be more careful.'

'It would help if you were in a relationship with a respectable girl. Don't pull that face. I know "respectable" is like the kiss of death to you, but we need the public to believe in you as one of the good guys, not a philanderer.'

'But I *am* a philanderer,' Travis pointed out.

'Then try to pretend you're not,' Denzil roared. 'You're an actor aren't you? So *act*!'

'Act what? Do I lie to the girl and pretend it's real? No way. That would be dishonest. Or do I tell her upfront that she's being made use of, then see her go straight to the press?'

Denzil groaned. 'Just get your life in order. There's a lot at stake, Travis. Think career. Think money.'

'All right. I'll think money.'

'And while we're on the subject—about tonight—'

'I'm not going to be at the dinner tonight,' Travis said firmly. 'There's been too much bad blood between Brenton and me.'

He escaped, breathing out hard in his exasperation and relief. As he headed down the corridor his cellphone shrilled. It was Pete, his agent.

'I suppose they've been onto you too?' Travis demanded.

'Denzil called me as soon as you'd gone,' Pete said. 'Apart from anything else, he's cross because you won't come to the dinner tonight.'

'And I told him the answer's still no,' Travis groaned.

There was to be a celebration dinner for Frank Brenton's sixtieth birthday. He was a studio big shot who'd invested a lot of money in the past and it was hoped he would put in more. Hence the big party.

'He can't stand me and I can't stand him,' Travis said. 'He pulled every string he could find to stop me being cast in the show, and he hates my guts because he failed. Best if we don't meet.'

'OK, OK. I told Denzil I'd raise it. But about the other thing, he just wants to be sure you understood the message.'

'But why have I got to be the only virtuous guy in Los Angeles?' Travis growled.

'Because it makes you different, and that difference puts a couple of extra noughts on the cheque. You haven't suddenly stopped caring for money and success, have you?'

'No way.'

'Then get a grip.'

'Am I supposed to live a totally moral life?' Travis demanded, aghast.

'No, I know you too well for that. But keep the fun stuff behind closed doors. In public, be seen only with ladies of impeccable morality. If they decided to replace you—well, there are several other actors just slavering to grab that part from you.'

He hung up, leaving Travis scowling at the dead phone.

'Grr!' he said.

He knew that both Pete and Denzil were right. Carelessly indulgent behaviour could imperil his career, and that was the last thing he wanted. He enjoyed the benefits of stardom too much. But what to do about it was a problem. The 'respectable' road definitely did not attract him.

But he couldn't say that openly without risking everything that mattered to him: his career, his reputation, his pride, the money that was pouring in. That money told the tale of a successful man;

not just to himself, but to others whose respect he cared for more than he wanted to admit.

'They think it's so easy,' he mused. 'If I *play* a guy who can soar above human temptations then I can be like that in real life. As if! All right, I was a bit careless with that girl in the nightclub, and I very nearly… But I didn't! It took a lot of self-control, but I didn't.

'If I was really a heavenly being, I could solve the problem in an instant. I'd turn the next corner and find the perfect solution just waiting for me. But in real life that kind of miracle doesn't happen. Ah well! Time to get to work. With luck, I might even get in touch with my virtuous side.'

He gave a wry laugh.

'Whatever that means.'

Charlene took a deep breath as she neared the studio entrance. It was now or never. In another moment she would get through that door as a member of a party privileged to tour the studio. Or perhaps someone would spot that she was a fraud; that she was here to see Lee Anton, the man with whom she was secretly in love, who had once seemed to love her, and whose feelings she desperately hoped to revive.

A pause in the queue gave her the chance to regard herself in a wall mirror. She'd taken trouble over her appearance and knew she looked as good as possible. Which wasn't very good, she thought sadly. Nature hadn't made her a beauty. Not exactly plain, but not exactly pretty either. Lee had called her 'Nice-looking' and praised her eyes.

'I like dark eyes,' he'd said, 'especially when they sparkle like yours.'

She'd clung to such remarks, and the fact that he sought her company rather than the beauties in the amateur dramatic society where they'd met. He was a professional actor, but back then his engagements were scarce and he'd been on the verge of chucking it in.

To pass the time he'd joined the amateur society, which was where they had met and quickly become attracted to each other. With her, attraction had soon become love, and she reached out to him with nothing held back. He'd responded eagerly, and the nights spent in his arms were the most joyful experiences of her life.

The play had been a triumph. She'd looked forward to the moment when he would ask her to marry him, and thought it had come when he said excitedly, 'Guess what! The most incredible thing—'

'Yes?' she asked breathlessly. Out of sight, she crossed her fingers. Here it came. The proposal.

Lee was almost dancing with joy.

'It's so wonderful!' he squeaked. 'It just shows that if you wait for the right moment—'

'And? *And? And?*'

'There was an American agent in the audience.'

'Wh...what?'

'He wants to take me on. He reckons he could get me a part in *The Man From Heaven*. They're looking for an English actor. Isn't that great? Isn't that the best thing you ever heard?'

'Yes,' she mumbled. 'Oh, yes, great.'

Two days later he'd left for Los Angeles.

'I'll stay in touch,' he'd promised.

And he had—after a fashion. There were emails, texts, the odd phone call, but no invitation for her to follow him. He was slipping away from her, and she couldn't let that happen. She had something urgent to tell him, something that couldn't be told on the phone.

Charlene had arrived three days ago, called him, leaving a message but receiving no response. Texts and emails went unanswered, and now she realised that he'd never given her an address. In the end she'd booked a place on the tour as the only way of seeing him.

She'd looked up the show online and learned the background story, and the role Lee was playing.

Up-and-coming English actor Lee Anton will be making his debut as Dr Franklin Baker, newly seconded to work at the Mercyland Hospital, where he rapidly becomes the friend and confidant of Brad Harrison, (played by Travis Falcon) and the only one who suspects his mysterious secret.

That morning she'd bought a newspaper, attracted by the headline—*HEAVENLY ANTICS, the latest startling story from the show everyone's talking about.*

But to her disappointment there was only the briefest mention of Lee. Most of the page was taken up by a photograph of a man sitting with a girl on his lap, his shirt open to the waist, her hand seductively caressing his bare chest. His face was only half visible and for a fearful moment she checked in case it was Lee. But it wasn't and she breathed again. It was only Travis Falcon.

Whoever he was, she thought, uninterested.

She knew she must be careful. Exposed to the glamorous temptations of Los Angeles, Lee was bound to have indulged himself, and she wouldn't spoil things between them by harsh judgements. That was in the past. When he'd heard her news everything would be all right, and only the future would matter.

But she was glad it wasn't Lee in the picture.

The queue was moving. Then she was inside, following the others in the guided tour that would end in the special privilege of being allowed to watch a scene being rehearsed. She paid only the slightest attention, while all the time her eyes wandered, seeking Lee.

Inside her head two voices were raging at each other.

He's dumped you. Why don't you face it?

And the other voice.

But he doesn't know about... When you tell him the news it'll make all the difference.

And then she saw him.

He was down the far end of a corridor, reading something on the wall. She tried to call him but her emotion caused her to choke. Suddenly he turned away and vanished around a corner. She began to run, not looking where she was going until she collided with an obstacle, felt two arms tighten around her and heard a man's voice say, 'Hey, steady there.'

'Let me go. I must catch him.'

Charlene wrenched herself free and ran along the rest of the corridor, turning the corner, then stopping abruptly, backing off, hand to mouth to silence the joyful cry that had been about to burst from her.

Now she could see him again: Lee, half turned away from her, hailing someone just out of sight.

'Where have you been?' he called. 'I've been looking for you. Come here and kiss me.'

The next moment a girl appeared from nowhere, throwing herself into his wide open arms, kissing him again and again between squeals of laughter, crying, 'Oh, darling, it's such wonderful news!'

He was laughing too, kissing her back, saying breathlessly, 'Hey that's right, give me a kiss…

and another…and another… Oh, I like that…oh, yes…oh, yes—'

He was lurching backwards under the girl's impact, until they both vanished around a corner. Charlene felt as though her heart had stopped dead. Not just her heart, but the whole world. That had been Lee. No—impossible. Yes—it had been Lee. No—yes—no—yes—*no*!

She turned wildly, knowing she had to get out of here. But her way was blocked by the man who'd been there before and who'd reappeared.

'I'm…I'm sorry—'

He put a friendly hand on her shoulder.

'Don't get upset. That guy's not worth it.'

'I—' She tried to speak normally, but only a choke would come.

'Don't cry,' he advised her.

'I'm not crying,' she said fiercely, although tears were streaming down her cheeks.

He didn't waste time arguing, just took out a clean handkerchief and dabbed her face gently.

'People kiss each other all the time,' he said. 'It doesn't mean anything, not in this place. Kissing is just like saying hello.'

She knew that what she'd seen was far more than

that, but he was trying to be kind, and she forced herself to be calm.

'Yes—yes—thank you. I'll stop bothering you now—'

'You're not bothering me. I just don't like to see you upset. Do you know him?'

'I thought I did—I mean, yes—no—'

He nodded, as though fully comprehending her confusion.

'I can't say I like him much myself,' he admitted. 'Are you one of his fans? You sound English. Did you follow him here?'

'No!' she said fiercely. 'Of course I didn't. What a thing to say!'

'Sorry, sorry. No offence. So you haven't lost your heart to him?'

'No!' she said violently. 'That would be just silly—mooning over a pretty face just because he's an actor.'

'It has been known,' he murmured wryly. 'But if you haven't, that's good. This is no place for people with hearts. What's your name?'

'Charlene Wilkins. Who are you?'

She sensed, rather than saw, a tremor of surprise go through him. 'What did you say?'

'I just asked your name. Have I seen you before somewhere?'

'Evidently not. My name's Travis Falcon. I work here.'

'Oh, yes—you're in the show, aren't you?'

His lips twitched with something that might have been amusement. 'That's one way of putting it. Now, let's get out of here. We've got time for a coffee before I start work.'

'No, I'm fine...fine—honestly—'

It was a lie. Appalled, she could feel herself on the verge of hysterics as the truth crashed in on her.

'Come on,' he said firmly. 'I'm not leaving you on your own in a strange place. Not given the state you're in.'

But to be alone was what she needed in case the screams rising within her broke out. When he reached for her she flailed madly to fend him off, and the next moment she heard a loud crack as her hand made contact with his face.

The sound was shocking and the way he rubbed his cheek told its own story. Charlene backed away, hands over her mouth, eyes wide with horror. But, incredibly, he wasn't offended.

'Hey, it's not that bad,' Travis said. 'No big deal.'

'It is. Oh, heavens, I hit you really hard. I didn't mean to— I'm sorry—'

'You will be if you don't let me buy you a coffee. Come on, no more arguments or I'll get tough.'

His tone was light but he held her arm in a no-nonsense grip. Nor could she have defied him now. All the strength seemed to have drained out of her. The next thing she knew, she was sitting at a table in the corner of the studio canteen.

'I'm going to the counter,' he said. 'Don't even think of escaping while I'm gone, or I'll get mad.' He gave her a kindly smile. 'I can be very nasty when I'm mad.'

He left her and she sat there, without the strength to move. She felt herself sagging everywhere—body, mind and heart. How had she been such a fool as to let it come to this? Plain, sensible Charlene, famed for her common sense! And she'd gone down like a row of ninepins.

Travis Falcon. Now she recalled that he was the star of the show. He didn't act like a star, proud and pompous. He hadn't been offended when she'd failed to recognise him, or even when she'd accidentally struck him. More like a nice guy than a star.

She dived into her bag and pulled out the newspaper with the picture of the man in the nightclub. As she opened it another picture fell out. It had been taken on a stage and showed a young man and a girl in nineteenth-century costumes, fervently clinging to each other. She took it with her everywhere.

'Here we are.' Travis's voice made her jump as he appeared with coffee and rolls. 'It's good to see you calmer. I was getting worried.'

'I'm really sorry about your face,' she said. 'I didn't mean to hit you.'

'I know you didn't.'

'It's not swelling, is it?' she asked, searching his face. 'If I've damaged you the studio will probably sue me.'

'Hey, do you think I'm some sort of a wimp to be so easily hurt? You're not the first girl to— Yeah, well, never mind that. Anyway, we're only rehearsing today, not shooting, so if you've disfigured me it won't matter until tomorrow.'

His comic self-deprecation was attractive, and her nerves eased enough to manage a shaky laugh, which made him regard her with approval.

'That's better. Now, let's talk. How do you come

to be here? I suppose you were looking for Lee?' She nodded and he said, 'Perhaps you should have warned him you were coming?'

'But I did, only…he doesn't seem to be getting his messages the last few days.'

Travis judged it best to maintain a tactful silence. He'd known Lee for only a few weeks and disliked him. Selfish, self-centred, indifferent to everyone else was how he would have described him. In the short time Lee had been in Los Angeles he'd raised the roof with his 'girly antics' as they had become known.

But he wouldn't say this to the young woman sitting beside him. There was no need. Clearly she was discovering it for herself.

'Do you know him well?' he asked.

'We've acted together.'

'You're an actress?'

'Not professionally. I work in a bank, but I do a lot of amateur acting. That's how I met Lee.'

'Hey, now I remember. There was a story in the papers—he hadn't had a job in a while, so he did some amateur stuff and an agent saw him.'

'That's right.' Charlene showed him the photograph. 'That's us.'

'What was the play?'

'A Midsummer Night's Dream.'

He raised his eyebrows. 'Lee played Shakespeare?'

'He was very good,' she said defensively. 'He was Demetrius, I was Helena.'

And Helena spent most of the play pursuing Demetrius, begging to know why he no longer loved her. Travis studied the picture, noticing the passionate adoration in her face and the impatience in his. How much of it was acting? Not much, he guessed, drawing on his knowledge of Lee.

He glanced at her. She was tall, with dark, straight hair, flowing casually over her shoulders. Not a beauty. Not even pretty in the strictest sense. Her features were regular but there was a slight touch of severity about her face that might warn people off, just at first, although it faded when she smiled, brightening her large dark eyes.

Intriguing, he thought. She didn't flaunt everything on the surface, but perhaps she might lure a man along a fascinating path of discovery. Or maybe not. Who could say? But she was exactly the kind of woman he doubted that Lee bothered with for long.

He knew a twinge of pity. He had an uneasy feeling that she was facing heartbreak.

A shadow appeared in the doorway and a woman strode in, looking around frantically.

'Oh, goodness!' Charlene said. 'I got in as part of a studio tour, and that's the leader, looking for me.'

The woman bore down on them, uttering words of concern and disapproval.

'I'm afraid it's my fault,' Travis said at once. 'Charlene is an old friend of mine and when I saw her here I persuaded her to spend the day with me.' He smiled at Charlene. 'You should have told me you were coming and I'd have rolled out the red carpet.'

'I didn't want to be a trouble,' she said, falling into character.

'You're never a trouble to me.' He turned back to the leader. 'You can safely leave her in my care.'

He accompanied the words with his warmest look and the leader melted.

'Oh, well…in that case I'll leave you to it.' She departed, but not before giving him a mystified look over her shoulder.

'You see?' Travis said to Charlene. 'No problem.'

'That was an incredible performance,' she said.

'You really fooled her. Thank you so much. And I won't be a nuisance. I'll go now.'

'No way. You just heard me say you were spending the day with me, so that's what you have to do.' He dropped his voice to a theatrical undertone. 'If you flee my company it looks bad. People will think I'm losing my touch.'

'And we can't have them thinking that,' she agreed.

'Right. Now it's time we went to the rehearsal.'

'We? Am I allowed?'

'You were going to go with the group.'

'Yes, but will they let me in on my own?'

'You won't be on your own. You're my guest, and you can do anything I say.'

He drew her to her feet, then crooked his arm for her to take.

'Time for our entrance,' he said.

CHAPTER TWO

WHEN they entered the rehearsal room the director raised his eyebrows, but a smile from Travis and his arm around Charlene's shoulder evidently answered all questions.

He saw her comfortably seated and flicked open the script. 'Which scene is it this morning?'

'The one where you try to talk Myra out of being in love with Dr. Baker,' the director said, 'and Baker overhears you—if those two would only turn up—ah, Lee, Penny, there you are!'

Charlene stiffened as Lee appeared in the doorway, with the girl she'd seen him with earlier. She turned her head but not quickly enough.

Lee had seen her.

He'd recognised her.

She tried to interpret his stunned look as pleasure. Now he would hurry across the floor to greet her.

But he stayed where he was, confused, troubled. Not delighted.

'Right, Lee,' the director said, 'we'll have a camera on you, to get a reaction shot. Travis, start at, "You should forget Dr Baker."'

They took their places and Travis began.

'You should forget Dr Baker. I know he's incredibly handsome, but looks don't really matter. Try to believe me. A man's face is the least of him.'

'Oh, they do matter, Dr Harrison, truly they do.' Penny sighed. 'He's so attractive that I can't help loving him.'

'But is he generous, affectionate, honest? Will he always put you first?'

'You mean is he dull and reliable?' she challenged.

Dr Harrison took her hands in his and spoke with feeling. 'I promise you, when you come to marry, dull and reliable is the best.'

'Fine,' the director said. 'Lee, you should try to look as though you've just had a terrible shock.'

Which he has, Charlene thought sadly.

The actress called Penny gave Travis a look of laughing camaraderie. '"Dull and reliable is the best,"' she teased. 'You sounded like you believed that nonsense.'

'I'm an actor,' Travis protested. 'I'm supposed to

talk nonsense convincingly.' He grinned. 'However little I believe it.'

'Well nobody ever accused you of being dull and reliable. That picture—'

'You didn't see it,' he said hastily. 'There's no picture.'

'If you say so.'

They rehearsed the scene several more times. Never once did Lee look in Charlene's direction, and perhaps Travis realised this too, because when there was a break he went over to him. Charlene couldn't hear what they said but she saw him take Lee's arm and draw him towards her. She noticed, too, the uneasy glance he gave Penny.

As Lee sat down next to her he managed a polite smile, but his words brought a chill to her heart.

'Fancy seeing you again.'

'Why do you sound surprised? I've been sending you texts—'

'My cellphone needs repair. Never mind. It's great to see you again. What are you doing here? Did you come to see Travis? I hear you're an old friend of his. *OK, I'm just coming!*'

The last words were called to Penny, who was

standing by the door, signalling him and mouthing a word that looked like *Lunch.*

'Old friend and good friend,' came a voice above Charlene's head. It was Travis, who'd been shamelessly eavesdropping. 'It made my day when you turned up here, Charlene. Now, make it even better and have lunch with me.'

His hand on her arm brooked no resistance. Not that she wanted to resist. She was too grateful to him. Lee gave her a meaningless smile and vanished out of the door with Penny.

There was no doubt that Travis had saved her dignity. All eyes were on them as he escorted her out of the studio, into the corridor, into the elevator, finally the canteen. Heads turned, people stared at him in the company of a girl nobody had seen before.

Charlene struggled to collect her thoughts. Lee's blank manner had told her everything she needed to know. But would that change when he heard her news? She had a terrible fear that it wouldn't.

'Thank you,' she said when they were sitting at the table. 'You saved me from looking a complete fool.'

'Don't call yourself a fool. That's just playing his game. Presentation is all important.'

'It'll take more than presentation to stop me looking pathetic,' she said in a tone of self-contempt. 'I came all this way for a man who isn't interested.'

'But nobody has to know. Smile at me. Let them see us enjoying each other's company. Go on, smile. More. That's better.'

She was aware of the crowded canteen, and even more aware of Lee and Penny sitting together.

Good, she thought defiantly. Now he knew she wasn't desperate for him.

'So you're a financial genius,' he said.

She made a face. 'That's what I used to think, but it seems not.'

'Hey, if you're good with figures then I'm impressed. I'm rubbish at them.'

'But it's possible to be good with figures and rubbish at everything else,' she said quietly. 'It doesn't make you good with people. I thought being good at the job was all I needed to get promoted, but the promotion went to some little doll-face who'd learned the job from me in the first place. When I protested I was told that they relied on me to keep an eye on her.'

'So you'd do the work and she'd get the credit?' Travis said sympathetically.

'And the company car. And the increase in salary. So I told them to forget it.'

'Good for you!'

She gave a brief laugh. 'I wasn't very clever. They offered me a bonus if I'd stay there, look after her and promise to keep quiet about "everything".'

'Meaning your boss and the girl he was sleeping with?'

'Right. I could have had it made, but I lost my temper. I was really violent. They say the building shook when I slammed out.'

'You?' he queried. 'Violent?'

'Well, you've already found that out, haven't you?'

'No, you didn't hit me on purpose. Pure accident. You seem so sedate, I just can't imagine you slamming out.'

He might have added that her clothes, hair and make-up told the same story: austere, severe, sober, stern, unyielding. There was nothing fiery about her. Not on the surface, anyway. But inside he guessed there was something else.

Perhaps Lee had tempted it out into the open,

which made it all the more strange that he was avoiding her.

'Well, I'm paying for it,' she said. 'If I'd been clever I'd have driven them to fire me, then claimed unfair dismissal and sued.'

'Admirable, but could you have driven them to fire you?'

'Maybe. People can be tricked into doing what you want.' She smiled. 'I expect you know that.'

'Sometimes,' he conceded. 'But I have a feeling I'm not as good at it as you.'

'Well, I wasn't good at it this time. First I lost my temper, then I realised I shouldn't have, and by then it was too late. I did everything by the virtuous book, but sometimes you can have too much virtue.'

'How true,' he murmured. 'So how did you find the cash to come here?'

'My grandparents paid. They brought me up since my parents died. They're lovely, adventurous people. Right now they're on holiday in Africa, looking for elephants. They said I could go with them but I chose to come here instead.'

'To find Lee?'

'Yes.'

'Where are you staying?'

'The Howley. Why do you shudder? Do you know it?'

'Not the hotel but that part of town. Depressing. I'd get out if I was you, find something better.'

He could have bitten his tongue out for his own tactlessness. Obviously she was making the money last, not knowing how long she would be here.

He took hold of her hand. 'Charlene, listen to me. Don't do anything crazy. It's not—'

'Well, this is nice!'

They both looked at the man who'd appeared just behind Travis. He was middle-aged, bulky, and his smile was a little too broad to be convincing.

'Hello, Denzil,' Travis said. 'Charlene, this is Denzil Raines, my boss.'

'None of that "boss" stuff,' Denzil said jovially. 'We're all friends here. So you're Charlene. I've been hearing about you. Nice to meet you. Hope you're having a good time. Travis, make sure you treat this lady well. All right, all right, I'll leave you two alone now.'

He took himself off, only turning at the last moment to give Travis a thumbs up sign and a beaming grin. Travis gave an inward groan.

'He seems nice,' Charlene observed. 'Is something the matter?'

'Everything's the matter. I'm sorry about that. Denzil is thinking how he can make use of you.'

'Of me? How?'

'The fact is—I've been a bit of an idiot, and if there's a disaster it'll be my own fault.' Caution made him stop there, but then he saw her face, kindly and understanding, as so few faces were in his world, and something drove him on to say, 'I went to a nightclub with some friends, and there was this girl—'

'The one that sat on your lap? Is that how they got the picture?'

He groaned. 'You've seen it? Yes, it was in the newspaper, wasn't it? I'm finished.'

'No, she's a bit blurred. You can sort of vaguely tell what she's up to, and the fact that she's hardly wearing anything, but the only face you can see is yours.'

'Yeah, me cuddling a nearly naked girl,' he groaned. 'Actually, I was fairly tipsy by then and I just sat there and let her…well… And I'm paying for it. I'm supposed to be virtuous in private as well as in front of the cameras.'

'And you're not,' she said sympathetically. 'Not below the waist, anyway.'

'Right,' he said, relieved to find her so mentally in tune.

'Well, I have the answer,' she said. 'The perfect solution to all your problems.'

'Tell me.'

'It's simple. All you have to do is take up residence in a monastery. There, your life will be unassailably righteous, your career will be protected, and the studio profits will be safe.'

He stared. 'You…you…' Then he saw the wicked glint in her eyes and joined in her laughter. 'You evil hussy!' he choked. 'I ought to…oh, but it was a good joke. You really had me scared for a moment.'

'Well, at least you're laughing,' she said.

'Yes, but it's no laughing matter. I could lose so much.'

Travis's phone rang. He answered quickly and seemed on edge.

'Mom, it's all right. Honestly. I can handle it. Stop worrying, I'll call you later.'

He hung up, looking harassed.

'She thinks I'm going to be brought down by

scandal,' he said. 'When she was making films nobody could have survived what's happening now.'

'A film actress? Hey, that's it. I thought you reminded me of someone, and now I can see. Julia Franklin.'

Julia Franklin had been a promising film actress some thirty years ago. For a while she'd shone brightly, and her old films were still shown on television.

'That's right,' Travis said. 'She's my mother. You've seen her?'

'One of her films was on television last night, and they're often shown in England. Everyone thought she'd go on to be a big star, but for some reason it didn't happen.'

'That's because she had me. Total disaster.'

'Did your father make her give up acting to be a full-time wife?'

'They weren't married. My father's English, a businessman who's always travelled a lot. Thirty years ago he was in the States to make some deal, met my mother briefly, and I'm the result.

'He was already married to his second wife, his first having chucked him out for playing around. My mother's film career was just taking off but he wanted her to throw it all away and follow him to England. Not for marriage, just to live as his mistress, be there when it suited him and keep quiet when it didn't.'

'I hope she told him what he could do with himself,' Charlene said indignantly.

'I'm proud to say that she did. In fact she did more than say it. If you met him you'd see a tiny little scar on his chin where she…let's say, put her feelings into action.'

'Do you mean *Amos* Falcon?' Charlene said suddenly. 'Hey, you're one of the Falcon dynasty.'

'In a sense,' Travis said so quietly that she barely heard.

'Amos Falcon was in the papers last week,' she went on excitedly, 'and there was a picture with this little scar—'

Travis groaned. 'All right, yes, but please forget it. I shouldn't have told you.'

Charlene began to chuckle. 'The journalist went on about that scar, how the "heroic" Amos Falcon confronted a robber and drove him off, at the cost of injury to himself.'

Travis gave a shout of laughter. 'Robber, my foot! Mom chucked an ashtray at him. She must have been a bit like you, losing your temper and storming out of the bank. She's got her violent side too. I reckon you two would like each other. She really scared my father. Not that he'd ever admit it, but after that things tended to be at a distance.'

'Do you mean you don't see him?'

'We meet occasionally, but we're not close. His second wife booted him out as well and he married a third time. I told Mom once that he ought to have married her—I was very young and naive in those days. She said she'd sooner marry the devil himself, except that the devil wouldn't be nearly so interesting as Amos Falcon.'

'He sounds a colourful character.'

'I believe his business enemies say the same. A falcon is a bird of prey, and he's known for preying on people. But enough about him. I must tell Mom the nice things you said about her. She'll be so thrilled that someone remembers her. What was the film they were showing?'

'Dancing on the Edge,' Charlene remembered.

'That's her,' Travis said at once. 'How often have I heard her say, "If it isn't on the edge, it isn't fun"?'

'She played the hero's sister, the one who was

always putting her foot in it, but everyone forgave her because she had that lovely cheeky grin.'

'True. And it's just how it is in real life. She blurts out all sorts of outrageous things, then says "Sorry, honey", and gives you such a smile that you have to forgive her.'

Charlene wondered if he realised that he had the same smile—mischievous, delightfully wicked. He was nice too, courteously paying her as much attention as if she'd been a raving beauty. Not like Lee Anton, she had to admit with an inner sigh.

As if reading her thoughts, Travis said suddenly, 'Why do you bother with him?'

'Maybe because I'm a fool,' she said lightly. 'We got close during the play—all those scenes we had together—'

'But they weren't love scenes,' Travis pointed out. 'Demetrius rejects Helena until the last minute—'

Charlene nodded. 'Saying things like, *I love thee not, therefore pursue me not.* But Helena won't get the message. She follows him saying, *Neglect me, lose me, only give me leave, unworthy as I am, to follow you.* What a twerp she is!'

She gave a grim laugh at herself. 'Listen to me, saying that. Follow him. That's exactly what I did.'

'But Helena won Demetrius in the end,' Travis pointed out.

'Only because someone cast a spell on him. It wasn't true love. It doesn't happen in real life. Oh, look, I'm sorry. I shouldn't be going on like this, making you listen. You've been really nice to me, although I can't think why, considering that I assaulted you.'

He'd been wondering that himself. He had a kind heart and often went out of his way to help people, but he didn't normally linger. Strangely, her clout across his face had been a turning point. Her horror and dismay had aroused his pity, making him want to defend her. He didn't fully understand it, but she ignited his protective instincts in a way that only one other person did. And that other person was his mother.

'I'll get out and stop bothering you—' she hastened to say.

'You're not bothering me.' He took her hand in both his and spoke gently. 'Look, I'll be honest. I have a selfish motive. I don't like Lee. I'm not sure why. There's just something about him that gets up my nose. It'll be a real pleasure to annoy him. You wouldn't be so hard-hearted as to deny me that pleasure, would you?'

It was a performance. The twinkle in his eyes revealed as much, and also the fact that he expected her to share the joke. And why not, she thought, since she gained from it?

'How could I be hard-hearted enough to deny you anything?' she said lightly, matching his theatrical fervour with her own.

He brushed his lips against her hand. 'That's good,' he murmured, 'because Lee's watching. No, don't turn your head. Just look at me. Try to seem entranced.'

She sighed, throwing back her head and giving him a glance of adoration, plus a brilliant smile.

'Well done,' Travis said. 'That'll teach him.'

'If he saw.'

'He did. He edged just closer enough to see everything. Trust me, I'm directing this production. Am I doing a good job?'

'They should give you an award,' she assured him, and he grinned. 'Is he still watching?' she asked.

'I'm afraid not. He's concentrating on Penny,

which makes sense because she's the female star of the show.'

'And she can do him a lot of good,' Charlene mused.

So Lee's interest in Penny was mostly professional. She would cling to that thought.

Travis read her mind and burst out, 'Forget him. He can't matter that much.'

'He does,' she said softly. 'But I can't talk about it.'

'All right, I won't press you. We'll talk some more tonight, over dinner.'

'I can't promise that—'

'You mean you want to stay free for him. But he's engaged this evening. He's got to go to this ghastly dinner they're giving for Frank Brenton. He and I can't stand each other so I won't be—*Wait a minute!*' He slapped his hand to his forehead. 'What am I thinking of? It's been staring me in the face all the time.'

'What is?'

He didn't answer but grasped her hand, looking round and calling, *'Denzil!'*

Denzil had appeared in the doorway and Travis hailed him loudly. He came straight over. Charlene felt Travis tighten his grip on her hand, urging her to say nothing.

'What's up with you suddenly?' Denzil asked, sitting down.

'I've been thinking about tonight, and maybe I was a little unreasonable. I'd like to attend that dinner after all, if they can accommodate me at the last moment.'

Denzil beamed. 'I don't think there'll be any problem about that,' he said.

'Fine, I'll want a table for two. Charlene will be my guest.'

Denzil nodded slowly, as though something had just become clear to him.

'Leave it to me. I'll fix it.' He vanished.

'So that's settled,' Travis said. 'Lee will be there tonight, so dress up to the nines. Let him know what he's missing.'

Her head was in a spin. Travis was making everything happen so fast, it was like being taken over by a whirling dervish. But a kindly dervish.

'It's nice of you to take so much trouble for me—' she began.

But he shook his head firmly. 'Let's be clear about this. I'm not being nice. I'm doing it for myself. You'll make me look respectable and that'll get them off my back. That's why I strong-armed you into it without asking your opinion first. Sheer bullying to get what I want. So don't praise me. I'm just being selfish.'

She regarded him fondly. 'So you're being selfish?'

'Horribly selfish.' There was a twinkling devil in his eyes. 'I don't know how you can stand me for a moment.'

'Neither do I,' she agreed. 'In fact, all I can say is—' she paused for dramatic effect '—if that's your idea of being selfish, I wish there were more selfish people in the world.'

'So you'll come?'

'Just try to stop me.'

'Fine, then it's time for you to go back to your hotel and prepare for tonight. Rick, my driver, will take you.'

A quick phone call to summon the car, then he escorted her out to where it was waiting with Rick behind the wheel. He was an elderly man with a good-natured face.

'Rick, this is Miss Wilkins, who'll be coming to the Brenton dinner with me tonight.'

Rick was astounded. 'But you said—'

'Never mind that. Things have changed. I want you to take her to her hotel now, and return there for her tonight. See you both later.'

He waved and stepped back as the car headed out into the traffic.

'Did I hear him right?' Rick called over his shoulder. 'The Brenton dinner?'

'Yes, what's the big deal? I know he'd planned not to go—'

'You can say that again. Travis gets on well with most people, but not that one. Brenton tried to ruin his big chance.'

'How?'

'His son's an agent, and he had his own candidate for the role. Brenton did all he could to talk the studio bosses out of giving it to Travis. He failed, so then he set out to get him fired. Spreading rumours, bad stories in the press. Didn't work. Since then it's been armed truce. Nobody expected Travis to go tonight. But now he's going so that he can take you. Lady, you must be really something!'

The habit of years made her begin modestly, 'Oh,

I don't think I'm—' But then her courage rose. 'As long as he thinks so, that's all that matters.'

'You said it!'

Charlene leaned back against the upholstery. Suddenly she was enjoying this, despite everything.

Rick delivered her to the hotel, waited while she collected her key, smiled and departed. She knew he'd regarded the surroundings with surprise. It was the kind of hotel described as 'budget', which meant that she had a dormitory room, shared with two other women. It wasn't ideal, but the place was clean and efficient, and she could connect her laptop to the Internet. This she did as soon as she arrived, looking up Travis Falcon, and growing more wide-eyed the more she learned of him.

The basics she already knew. He was the son of Julia Franklin and Amos Falcon of the international Falcon dynasty. But now she learned that he'd started his career on the stage, graduated to tiny roles in films before being pounced on by the studio and cast in the series.

There were hints that his private life was colourful. He was a playboy who never seemed to stay with one girlfriend for long. He indulged in flirtations, not love. But until now his liveliness had stayed within acceptable bounds. The nightclub picture marked the start of a new phase, and Charlene could see why his bosses were concerned.

Studying the photographs, she had to admit that he was the handsomest man she'd ever seen. And the most charming. It wasn't a matter of looks. His face had a magical 'something' that spoke of a lust for life, a readiness to dive in anywhere and try anything. He was filled with humour, sometimes bawdy, sometimes cheeky.

Actually, she mused, *the man from heaven can be a bit of a devil. Good for him!*

She remembered how he'd treated her that afternoon—kindly, gently, with warmth and understanding, and she thought she could see those things in his face. Most people would have missed them, she reckoned, but she knew better.

All right, he was making use of her. But in a way she was making use of him. It was a fair bargain. Now it was time to prepare for the evening in such a way that she would be a credit both to herself and Travis.

I ought to be grateful, she thought. *Lee's turned his back on me—*

But the next moment she clasped her hand across her stomach, still slim despite her suspicions.

But things may change, she told herself. *I won't know anything until I've told him.*

She refused to believe that he could have dumped her completely after what they had shared. There was still hope.

CHAPTER THREE

A QUICK visit to a nearby hairdresser and her dark locks were transformed, becoming curled and lush. The blue satin dress was elegant, closely fitting a slender figure that many women would have envied.

And yet there was something missing. Honesty forced Charlene to admit that. Whatever the magical 'extra' was, she knew she didn't have it. She looked pleasant, but not special.

Nor could she recall ever being really special to anyone in her life. Even her mother.

Her father had been mostly absent, more absorbed by his work than his family. He'd died when she was five, and her mother had remarried a year later. She and Mark, her stepfather, had been reasonably affectionate in an undemonstrative sort of way, but she'd sensed even then that they meant more to each other than she did to either of them. Mark had a son, James, by a previous marriage, who lived with his mother. Mark had been immensely proud of him, often speaking of him in a way that made Charlene feel that she herself didn't really exist. Even her mother, anxious to please her husband, had sometimes seemed to value James more than her own daughter.

Once she'd overheard them discussing the idea of another baby.

'It would be nice to have a daughter,' Mark had remarked.

'We've got Charlene,' her mother had pointed out.

'Yes, but—you know what I mean. A real daughter—ours.'

She had crept hastily away and never mentioned what she had heard. The casually unkind words, *a real daughter*, haunted her ever after.

When she was fifteen they had taken a holiday together. Just the two of them.

'Can't I come?' Charlene had pleaded.

'Darling, it's our anniversary,' her mother had said. 'Mark and I need to be alone. You can understand that, can't you?'

Of course she could understand. She'd always understood why she wasn't a priority.

So they had gone without her, and never returned. Everyone said how lucky it was that she hadn't been on the plane when it crashed, but haunting her grief was the knowledge that she hadn't been wanted.

Her mother's parents had taken her in. They had no other children or grandchildren, and they consoled themselves by lavishing affection on Charlene. In their warmth she blossomed, and much of the pain was eased. She had two people to love, and she knew that they loved her.

But the knowledge of having been second best never quite left her. Her stepbrother was never in touch, which made her sad because it would have been nice to have a big brother.

She'd come to understand that she was moderate in all things: moderate-looking, nothing special; moderately talented, with skills that were efficient rather than glamorous. Her bank employers praised her with the words, 'We need good back-room staff.' And she felt that this was where she belonged. In the back room—of work, of life, of love, of everything. The spotlight was for others.

She had boyfriends, but none seemed to last long. The one she'd cared for most had turned out to be using her to get close to her best friend. Charlene had been a bridesmaid at their wedding, which had seemed to her to be a gloomy portent for the future.

Always the bridesmaid, never the bride, she'd thought, gazing at her reflection on the day.

But on the stage it was different. In the spotlight another side of her came to life, and she revelled in it. Her scenes with Lee had inspired the producer to say, 'You two really make something fizz between you. Keep going.'

And something had happened, something that continued when they'd left the stage, that took them into each other's arms, then into the same bed. It was her first experience of passion, and she rejoiced.

Lee hadn't rejoiced. He'd been troubled.

'Look, I'm sorry,' he'd said hastily. 'I didn't know you weren't…that you hadn't…I mean…'

'I guess I was waiting for you,' she'd said softly, but that had seemed to trouble him even more.

She'd thought how nice he was to be concerned for her. The other thought, that he simply hated responsibility, was one she avoided.

But soon it would have to be faced. This afternoon he'd seen her at her dullest. Tonight she would present a face that reminded him of another time. And they would talk.

Her two room-mates, both pleasant young women, applauded her appearance.

'Got a decent guy escorting you?' one of them asked.

'Travis Falcon.'

They whistled, as though impressed. But in the mirror she caught the look they exchanged, which said plainly that she was fantasising. Nobody who had to stay in this run-down hotel could ever attract such a glamorous escort.

She didn't really blame them for not believing her. She barely believed it herself. Perhaps it really was a fantasy, and Travis would fail to turn up, leaving her abandoned.

In fact he was downstairs at that moment, looking around with horrified eyes. It was as bad as Rick had warned him. He hastened upstairs and knocked on her door.

It was opened by a young woman whose face registered total astonishment at the sight of him.

'Is Charlene here?' he asked.

'Yes, she… Hey, Charlene—' She turned back

to Travis. 'Are you really…really…?' She seemed about to faint.

'Yes, really,' he assured her, stepping into the room and offering Charlene his arm. 'Shall we go, my lady?'

To his delight, she slipped into the role easily, taking his arm and declaring, 'Thank you, kind sir.'

From the way the other two stared at them it was clear that Charlene's standing had rocketed. They came out into the corridor and followed the couple with longing eyes until they had vanished. Then they threw themselves into each other's arms and screamed.

Charlene tried, unsuccessfully, to control her mirth.

'Glad you find it funny,' Travis said as they settled into the back seats of the car.

'It's myself I'm laughing at, not you.' She chuckled. 'Did you see their faces? A woman who can claim Travis Falcon as an escort is a woman to be reckoned with.'

'Even if she's poor enough to stay in this neighbourhood,' he said. 'You should have something better. Bad characters hang out here, and they'll be very interested in that bracelet you're wearing. Did Lee give it to you? If so, I commend his taste.'

'No, it belongs to my grandmother.'

'Are you wearing anything from him?'

She shook her head. There had been no gifts from Lee.

'Then put this on,' he said, holding up a necklace.

Even in the dim light of the car she could see that it was a glorious, expensive piece. She felt in a daze as he fixed it around her neck, his fingers touching her softly. She was going to a glamorous occasion, escorted by the most handsome man she'd ever seen, and she was determined to enjoy it. Whatever the future held, she would make the most of tonight.

She had only the vaguest notion of their destination, and her eyes widened as they reached Sunset Boulevard, in the heart of the most glamorous part of a glamorous city.

'Where is this dinner being held?' she asked.

'At the Stollway Hotel.'

Her jaw dropped. The Stollway was among the most lush, lavish and expensive places in town. Next moment, they were nearing the entrance and she could see the flashing lights, the cars crowding in to disgorge gorgeously dressed men and women onto the broad red carpet.

'I had no idea it would be like this,' she gasped.

'The PR department has made the most of it,' Travis said.

'But I thought it would just be a restaurant. This place is so big and…that crowd…it's like a premier.'

'Good. So there'll be a lot of people to see the story we're trying to tell them. They'll know that you don't need Lee Anton, because you can have any guy you want, just by snapping your fingers. And they'll see that I only like nice girls.'

While she struggled for words, his face softened, his eyes became pleading.

'I guess I wasn't quite straight with you. I should have told you everything but I was afraid you'd say no, and I really need to do this. You can get me out of trouble as nobody else can.'

She remembered how he'd cast his protective mantle over her that afternoon. But for that, she'd be back in the hotel now, fighting back tears of rejection.

'But do you think I'm up to it?' she said. 'It's so scary.'

'We'll do it together. Don't be afraid. Just smile and make it look as though it was the most natural thing in the world to you, and you love every minute.'

He put his hands on either side of her face, looking deep into her eyes. 'Give the performance I know you can give.'

Suddenly she was inspired. There was a time for ducking out and a time for making the most of things, and this was definitely the second.

'As long as you're there, giving me directions,' she said. 'Let's do it.'

'That's the spirit. I knew I could rely on you. Now, here comes our grand entrance.'

The car stopped. Cheers erupted from the crowd as they saw Travis emerge, smiling, waving, then reaching in for her. She took his hand and he drew her out into the spotlight.

He was playing his part perfectly, leading her slowly along the carpet so that everyone could get a good view of her quiet, restrained appearance. A gentle tug on her hand and he drew her around to the other side, just in case there was anyone who hadn't seen how modest and ladylike she was.

Charlene smiled, turned to meet his eyes, and almost gasped at the adoring look he was giving her. If she hadn't known better, she could almost have believed him about to fall on his knees and worship her.

What an actor! she thought.

He drew her hand to his lips and the cheers rose around them. She lowered her eyes, apparently overcome, and felt him draw her close.

'Well done,' he murmured in her ear. 'Keep it up.'

As they approached the huge main doors there was a flicker of interest from behind them. Turning, they saw another car arrive, the door open and Lee emerge, accompanied by Penny. Their arrival caused a small commotion but nothing like the agitation that had greeted Travis. As they danced along the carpet three photographers dashed out to get closer shots.

Lee turned his head, laughing, preening in the spotlight. But his smile died as the photographers passed him by to surround Travis and Charlene. She had a brief glimpse of Lee's face, aghast, astounded, chagrined. Then Travis swept her into the building.

Inside, there was more of the same as they made their way to the huge restaurant at the back of the hotel. It was called Aladdin's Cave, and decorated with a magical theme. Brightly coloured lanterns hung from the ceiling, elaborate pictures decorated the walls and everywhere there was the glitter of gold.

They were escorted to a table for two, where he settled her with every attention and said, 'Let's have something to drink.'

'Orange juice for me, please.'

'This is an evening for champagne,' he protested.

'Orange juice,' she said firmly. 'Or sparkling water.'

He was silent a moment, but then nodded and made the order. He asked no further questions, but she had a sense that he understood why she wouldn't touch alcohol.

Denzil bustled over, rubbing his hands with delight, paid Charlene extravagant compliments and then bustled away. People were arriving slowly, waving at Travis, looking curiously at Charlene before flaunting themselves before each other, all putting on performances. For the moment it was still quiet enough to talk.

'You've saved my neck, you know that?' Travis said. 'All those pictures they took of us outside. I have a career again.'

'Just like that?'

'It can happen that way in this city. Here today, gone tomorrow, back again the day after.'

'Don't you ever find the life exhausting?'

'Well, I do end up living on edge a lot of the time, but it can feel worth it.'

'I suppose success is wonderful.'

'Yes. Not that I've been a success long enough to know very much. But it matters to me to achieve everything I can, just to stop my father disowning me.'

'But surely you don't need him? You're independent.'

'I meant disowning me in spirit.' Travis gave a brief laugh. 'It's odd isn't it? I disapprove of Amos, sometimes I even dislike him. But I still hate the feeling that I'm the one on the outside of the family. He despises me for not being like him, the way my brothers are.'

'All of them?'

'Mostly. Darius is a big man in finance, just like Amos. He's been hit by the credit crunch, and now he's living on Herringdean, an island off the south coast of England that one of his debtors used to pay him off. He started out hating it, but he came to love it. Falling in love with a local girl helped. I was at their wedding a few weeks ago and if ever two people were crazy about each other it's those two.'

'You sound as though you envy them.'

'In a way I do. It's nice to know your final destination, and be able to reach it. Darius has been married before and it didn't work out, but he's safe with Harriet. Plus his first wife likes her, even encouraged them to marry because their two children like her as well.'

Charlene recalled him talking about his father and all the children Amos had by different women. His brother's arrangement sounded so much happier that she began to understand the touch of wistfulness in his voice.

He can't really be jealous, she thought. *An ordinary domestic set-up. Many people would call it boring, but the great star actually wishes...no, that's just the sort of thing he'd say in interviews. I'm imagining things. Shut up, Charlie.*

'What did you say?' Travis asked, staring at her suddenly.

'Nothing.'

'I thought you whispered, "Shut up, Charlie".'

'Did I say that out loud? Oh, heck!'

'You actually call yourself Charlie?'

'When I'm trying to remember to be sensible. It's not easy in a place like LA. Common sense seems the last thing you can manage, and actually the last thing you want.'

'I know the feeling,' he said wryly.

'So your brother's settled for common sense?'

'That's not what Darius calls it. To him it's finding out what his life is really all about.'

'And it's not just about money?'

'Not any more. It was once but that was his "Amos" side. Now he's found something else and the Amos side is having to stand back.'

'I'll bet Amos doesn't like that.'

'Too right. He tried to stop their marriage, but failed. Mind you, Darius will climb to the financial top again. It's in the Falcon genes. Marcel is like Amos too, except for being half French. He makes his money from hotels. He's got a big, glamorous place in Paris and he's recently bought another one in London to "extend his empire". Amos loves that. To him, that's how a Falcon should think, in terms of empire.'

'Perhaps you need to play a Roman emperor,' Charlene mused. 'How about Julius Caesar?'

'Better still, Nero,' he said, catching her mood. 'Or Caligula.'

'But Nero was a tyrant,' Charlene objected.

'Great. That makes him a true Falcon.'

'And Caligula was mad. Wouldn't your father hate that?'

'Not if it made money.'

They laughed together.

'Haven't you got two other brothers?'

'Yes, there's Leonid, who's Russian and lives in Moscow. We don't know a lot about him, but he must be successful because Amos always speaks of him with respect. Jackson's different. He's a naturalist. He's written books and has a television series about wildlife all over the world.'

'That doesn't sound like it makes him a million-aire.'

'No, he's not. But Amos respects him, nonetheless, because the world knows him as a "serious man" doing a "serious job". I just "flaunt myself for the press", but Jackson "defends the environment" and that elevates the name Falcon, even if not in business.

'He actually told me once that I should change my name because he didn't want to be connected with someone "prancing around for the cameras".'

'Your father doesn't want you to be called after him?' she asked, aghast.

'He despises what I do. He was furious when I wouldn't take a different name.'

'No wonder you feel shut out,' she said sympathetically.

'Not by the others. I get on fine with my brothers, what little I see of them. But I think Amos is just hanging on in the hope that one day I'll change into a mini-Amos.'

'You could always act it,' she suggested.

'Not if I want to stay sane,' he said hastily. 'This way, at least I know who I am. Or I would, if people didn't keep wanting me to put on a performance in private as well as in front of the cameras.'

'You poor soul.' She sighed. 'The burdens of fame. Just think of all those unemployed actors out there who must be so grateful they don't have your problems.'

He scowled for a moment, but then relaxed and squeezed her hand, smiling ruefully.

'Yeah, right. I must be coming across as a bit of a wimp, eh? It's your fault. You're such a tempting, sympathetic shoulder to cry on that I gave in. But no more.' His voice deepened and he assumed a haughty mien. 'From now on, just macho authority and stern resolve.'

'Ouch, please, no!' she said. 'I can't stand men like that.'

'Neither can I,' he admitted. 'Perish the thought that I should ever be one of them.'

'Nothing could be less likely,' she reassured him.

He met her eyes in a look of total understanding, and suddenly she had the strangest feeling of having known him all her life. It made no sense but instinctively she was his friend, and she sensed him becoming her friend.

'You see right through me, don't you?' he said, amused.

'I guess I do. Do you mind?'

'Not a bit. Know what? I think we're going to get on really well.'

'Me too. Here's to a great evening.'

They raised their glasses, and were about to clink when a voice cut in between them like a knife.

'Well, well! Look who's here.'

Looking up, Charlene saw a tall, hard-faced, middle-aged man, regarding them coldly. She heard Travis groan, then say, 'Charlene, this is Frank Brenton. Brenton, this is Miss Charlene Wilkins.'

Brenton flickered cool, angry eyes over her, nodded, then spoke to Travis in a rough voice. 'Some people have a gift for escaping from awkward situations. I congratulate you. You got away with it this time, but there'll be others. That's guaranteed.'

'Nothing's guaranteed,' Travis said.

'I think you'll find you're wrong. You go about inviting trouble, Travis, and such an invitation always gets accepted.'

There was frank dislike in his eyes. His glance at Charlene was almost insulting, and an incredible suspicion came to her, making her temper flare.

She slipped her arm about Travis's neck, leaning her head against him.

'You never know what life holds next,' she said

sweetly. 'Of course, some people think they do, but then they get taken by surprise.'

'Oh, I don't think I'm going to be surprised.'

She met his eyes. 'Nobody ever does until it happens.'

'Perhaps you'll be the one surprised.'

She shook her head. 'That won't happen, because I believe the worst of people.' She fixed him with a hard, steady gaze before saying, 'The very worst, more than most people would ever dream of, because I have a nasty, suspicious nature. But, like you say, we'll just have to wait and see.'

Brenton seemed on the verge of answering, but then he thought better of it, scowled and walked away.

Travis stared at her in astonishment. 'What the blue blazes was that all about?'

'You don't know? You haven't guessed?' she asked regarding him wryly.

'Did you just do what I thought you did? You drove the enemy off and now he's taking cover.'

'I think he might be more the enemy than you realised. That girl in the night club; did she really just appear out of nowhere?'

'Well, yes, it was a stag night and… Hey, what… are you saying—?'

'That he fixed it? I don't know. But it's possible, isn't it? He knew you'd be there, it would have been easy for him to arrange.'

'You mean he—?'

'First the girl, then the photographer. Was it just chance that they appeared? Didn't you ever wonder?'

He shook his head. 'I just thought it was one of those things,' he said.

'Travis, wake up! You live in the middle of this city, where people must be playing tricks on each other all the time. You're far too trusting. Now I've met him, I can see that he's exactly the kind of man who'd do that.'

'All in five minutes? You saw it and I didn't.' His shoulders sagged. 'And I think of myself as worldly wise.'

He sounded depressed and she smiled at him fondly. There was something about Travis that was the complete opposite of worldly wise, and which drew her towards him. He was, as he'd said, too trusting. In this sophisticated city, that part of him was dangerously vulnerable.

'Thank goodness for you,' he said. 'What would I do without you?'

'For the moment you don't have to. You've got a big sister keeping an eye out for you.'

He grinned and squeezed her hand. 'I'd offer to be your big brother, but I guess I'd keep tripping over things and making a mess of it.'

'Big brother sounds nice. I'll watch out to see you don't trip up too much. Hey, look at him now.'

Together they watched the long table at the head of the room. It was slightly raised, making it easy to see Brenton taking his place. People were waiting for him, including a man with a similar face.

'Travis, that man who's slapping Brenton on the shoulder—'

'His son.'

'You mean the agent? Rick told me about them.'

'That's right. And the guy with them is the actor Brenton wanted to see cast instead of me.'

'There's a faint likeness. He's not Brenton's son as well, is he?'

'Not officially, but there are rumours. I guess they're probably true.'

'So that's why they're so determined to discredit you. You watch out. He as good as said that he'll try something else. Just don't make it easy for them.'

'No, I won't—now I can see it—'

He rubbed his eyes, then looked at her again closely and spoke in a voice of awed discovery. 'I'm beginning to think meeting you was the best thing that's ever happened to me.'

CHAPTER FOUR

TRAVIS rubbed his eyes again. 'I guess you just never know what's around the corner, and... Charlene?'

But he'd lost her attention. Her gaze was fixed on the far side of the room where Lee was entering with Penny on his arm. They were smiling at the world and at each other, looking around the room, then back to each other. A photographer positioned himself before them and they twisted and turned as expected, before making their way to their table.

Travis observed Charlene, noting how she never moved, but sat clasping the stem of her glass with tense fingers. At last she relaxed and looked away. He took her hand in his and squeezed it gently. She squeezed back. There was no need to say anything.

The evening began. A lavish banquet was served to the long table up high at the end of the room and the twenty smaller tables spread out around the room. As she ate the delicious food Charlene wondered what had possessed her to speak as she had done. She'd implied to Travis that she was here for him and only for him, to take care of him and be 'big sister' to his 'big brother'.

But that couldn't happen. She was here for Lee. Soon they would talk, she would tell him her news, they would become a couple and her usefulness to Travis would end.

She searched the room. Lee was sitting with Penny, not far away but half obscured by other tables. She watched him, willing him to see her. Yes, now his glance had turned her way. But no, now it had turned away again.

'Charlene,' Travis said quietly. 'Are you all right?'

'I'm fine,' she said, smiling at him, giving the performance they had agreed. 'It's going to be a really wonderful evening.'

He'd seen what had happened. He understood what she was doing, and his admiration grew.

As the meal neared its end people rose and drifted from table to table.

'Come on,' Travis said, taking her hand and drawing her across the floor, calling, 'Lee, good to see you here. And Penny. You look lovely, darling.'

Penny received his kiss with delight, glad to give the show's star her whole attention, leaving Lee no choice but to talk to Charlene.

'Fancy seeing you again,' he said brightly as she sat beside him.

'You speak as though you never expected to see me again,' she said. 'But we weren't going to leave things there, were we?'

'I didn't mean to dash off the way I did. Things just happened suddenly.'

'I know. I'm glad for you. But I had to see you again because…after we were so fond of each other…'

'Yes, we were. I remember that well, but…life moves on. Things are so different now that it wouldn't have been fair for me to try to drag you in, and—'

'But you didn't drag me. I'm here because I wanted to see you.'

'That's sweet of you, but I hate to think how much it must be costing you. This town is so expensive.'

'Well, it is a bit, yes, but—'

Surely he would offer to help her with the cost? She waited for the words.

'Look, Charlene, perhaps—'

'Yes?'

'Perhaps you should go home. You can't afford it and I shall worry about you.'

'You don't need to worry about me.'

'Well, I know that really. You were always the strong one, weren't you? Nothing happens that you can't cope with.'

His smile was like a steel mask.

'Lee, I need to talk to you. There's something—'

'Attention, everybody!' The cry came from the top table. 'Can you all return to your seats, please? The best part of the evening is about to start.'

Charlene sat still, feeling as though dead weights were dragging her down, until Travis's gentle hands drew her to her feet. He paused to smile back at Penny, saying, 'I'll claim that dance later. Keep it for me.'

'Oh, lovely!' she cried.

Images flickered through Charlene's consciousness. Penny, thrilled by attention from Travis, Lee disgruntled because she was focusing on another man.

At their table, Travis drew out her seat and ushered her into it, as theatrically attentive as a servant. He was doing it for her, she knew. Just as he'd fixed it so that she could talk to Lee, he would fix it again by dancing with Penny. But it would all be for nothing. Lee was embarrassed to see her. He'd made that very plain.

She should never have come here.

Charlene laid her hand softly over her stomach, then moved it away quickly, unaware that Travis was watching her with kindly, troubled eyes.

The speeches began. Denzil Raines praised Brenton to the skies, wished him happy birthday and presented him with a costly gift. More gifts, more speeches. Brenton accepted it all with an evident sense of entitlement. Charlene reckoned this was a man used to getting his own way, who didn't easily give up.

It was time for the dancing. Travis claimed Penny at once, thus freeing Lee to talk to Charlene. But when she approached his table it was empty.

It offended her pride to go searching for him, but pride was something she couldn't afford right now, so she looked around until she saw him deep in conversation with Denzil. There was no way she could interrupt him now, as he must have known. Heavy-hearted, she began to return to her table.

'Got a few minutes to spare for me?'

Brenton was standing there, a grim smile on his face.

'So Travis has dumped you already, has he?' he asked. 'That's what you must expect. He's just making use of you. When you've served your purpose you'll be out.'

'And you know all about using people to serve a purpose, don't you, Mr Brenton. Who do you think you're fooling?'

'And just what does that mean?'

'It means exactly what you're afraid it means. I know what you did. You're not so on top of the situation as you think you are.'

'Everything all right?' That was Travis's voice. The dance had ended and Penny had already gone in search of Lee.

'Everything is wonderfully all right,' Charlene declared. 'Mr Brenton has just made his meaning plain to me, and I've made my meaning plain to him.'

Very deliberately, she stepped closer to Travis and slid her arm around his neck. Her message was plain. Brenton could do his worst. Travis was under her protection now and everyone had better remember that.

Travis reacted on cue, putting his arm around her waist, drawing her close, echoing her message. Brenton made a face and walked away.

'Let's go outside for a while,' Travis said.

'Oh, yes,' she said gratefully. 'Let's get away from here.'

The hotel garden was full of trees hung with lights. As they strolled beneath them, music reached them from a distance.

'I'm not sure exactly what I walked into,' Travis said, 'but I reckon you just sent the enemy packing for the second time tonight. Was he giving you trouble?'

'Not as much as I gave him. He warned me that you'd dump me when I'd served my purpose.'

'I won't get the chance. You'll dump me first. Did you fix things with Lee?'

He sensed her reluctance to answer. 'Not really,' she said. 'We need another meeting.'

'And will that be any different?' he asked ironically. 'No, no, I shouldn't have said that. I'm sorry, *I'm sorry*!'

'Probably not,' she admitted. 'I can't kid myself

that he was glad to see me, but I can't leave things as they are.'

'Well, one thing will definitely change. You're not staying in the Howley. You must move in here.'

'I couldn't possibly afford this place,' she protested.

'But I can. You've helped me, and now I'm going to help you. You won't even ask me about the bill.'

'Won't I?'

'No. That's an order. You're moving in here and living like a star. It's the only way to be taken seriously in this town. We'll book your room now, then collect your things from the Howley. That's settled. No argument!'

She surveyed him tenderly. 'So you really can do macho?'

'Well, sometimes—if someone else writes the script. Come on, let's get this sorted.'

A hundred pairs of eyes watched as they left the restaurant, arms about each other's waists. At the reception desk there were more curious eyes to see Travis order the room.

'I want the best suite you have,' he said. 'Make sure it's ready in an hour. And please give this note to my driver, who's in the canteen at the back, so that he'll know I want the car.'

'Are you sure you should be leaving?' she asked as they headed out of the hotel. 'Perhaps you should stay for the rest of the celebration.'

'The things I'm celebrating have nothing to do with this place. And I'm not letting you out of my sight in case you vanish,' he said, looking alarmed. 'You saved me from disaster.'

As if to prove it, Denzil appeared, smiling to see them together, and waved them on their way.

'See what I mean?' Travis said. 'That was the official seal of approval. Ah, there's Rick!'

When they were settled in the car and moving off, Rick said over his shoulder, 'I watched the arrivals on TV. You sure looked good.'

Travis grinned and gave Charlene a thumbs up. She returned the gesture.

At the Howley, Travis accompanied her up to her room, waited while she packed, then picked up her luggage and headed downstairs.

'Oh, no!' she said, in dismay. 'The desk is closed. How can I pay my bill if there's nobody there?'

'You've already paid the bill,' Travis said.

'But how—?'

'Rick saw to it while we were upstairs.'

'But how did he know to—? That note you sent him. You told him to—'

'Let's get out of here,' he said hastily.

'You went behind my back.'

'I didn't want to waste time arguing, and I still don't. Come on, let's go.'

As they went out she said, 'Of course I'll pay it back. How much do I owe you?'

'Just get in the car.'

'How much?'

'Get in the car!'

On the journey back she tried to feel indignant, but it was impossible. The feeling of being protected was like a draught of magic. Even her sadness about Lee faded before it.

'You know what you are, don't you?' she murmured.

'Something terrible, I guess.'

'A male chauvinist porker!'

He beamed. 'That's the nicest compliment anyone's ever paid me!'

Rick roared with laughter over his shoulder.

They reached the hotel to find that the revelries

had ended and the place was quietening down for the night. Travis escorted her to her suite.

It had a luxurious bathroom, a huge bed and vast windows overlooking Sunset Boulevard. Charlene stared, trying, unsuccessfully, to imagine her ordinary self in these palatial surroundings. But she made no protest. Clearly Travis had a plan in mind, and now she must leave everything to him.

She knew that some people would say this was foolish. How could she draw Lee back to her by being seen with Travis?

But in her heart she knew that a few short hours had changed everything between herself and Lee. He hadn't missed her and didn't want her. Only a woman determined to delude herself could think otherwise. He was ambitious, which was one reason for escorting Penny, who was more established and could inspire the interest of the press.

But the really big star was Travis. It was he who made headlines, and the fact that Charlene had apparently secured his interest had made Lee gape with astonishment.

She didn't know what the future held, but having Travis as her champion saved her from humiliation and she would cling to him.

As though he'd read her thoughts, Travis said, 'Don't worry. If Lee comes knocking I'll fade into the background.'

'I wonder if he will,' she mused.

'And if he did, would that make you happy? Do you really want him?'

'Let's say I'm seeing him with new eyes, but... it might be complicated—'

He put his hands on her shoulders. 'Are you pregnant?' he asked quietly.

She looked up and the misery in her face made him catch his breath.

'I don't know for sure,' she said desperately. 'When I was late I did a pregnancy test, and it was positive. But then someone told me that shop-bought pregnancy tests aren't always one hundred per cent accurate so I did another one and that was negative. But I'm still late. Perhaps I should have waited until I was more certain before I came here, but I was so happy, and I thought he might be happy too.'

She choked off into silence. Travis wasted no more words. Instead he drew her close, his arms around her in a warm hug.

'I've got a doctor friend who'll help you,' he said.

'We'll get a definite yes or no. Don't worry. I'll take care of everything. Now, I'm going. Go to bed and get some sleep. I'll call you in the morning.'

He placed a gentle kiss on her cheek, and left.

She went to bed but couldn't sleep. Her thoughts seemed to be fighting each other. One saying that she'd expected better from Lee. The other asking if it was really such a surprise? Hadn't she, in her heart, known that he wouldn't welcome her?

She laid her hands over her stomach, wondering what she should tell him; wondering if there was anything to tell.

Her eyes were closing when a soft knock at the door made them open wide. Throwing on a robe, she hurried to answer, half expecting Travis.

But it was Lee who stood there, looking anxious.

'Are you alone?' he asked.

'Quite alone,' she said, standing back to let him in. 'What else did you expect?'

'Well…he might be with you.'

'He?'

'Travis. They say he never passes up a chance.'

'Well, you're wrong,' she said with a touch of anger. 'I came to Los Angeles to see you.'

'Yes, but after the way he's been haunting you

tonight, I thought… Well, you've really got his attention.'

'Lee did you come here to insult me, because—?'

'I'm not insulting you. That guy lives in the spotlight, and if he's interested in you then you've got the spotlight as well. This is LA. These things matter.'

'And you wouldn't mind me sharing his spotlight?' she demanded. 'Even though you and I have some unfinished business?'

'I thought we sorted that out earlier.'

'Then you must think it was very easily sorted. We made love, Lee, and sometimes that can produce results. Have you thought of that?'

The sheer blank horror in his face answered every possible question.

'Are you saying…? You mean you're…? Are you sure?'

'No, I'm not sure. It isn't definite yet.'

'Phew! So things might still be all right.'

'That depends on what you mean by all right.'

'Charlene, I swear I didn't want to leave you in trouble. If the worst comes to the worst I'll help you fix it. There are places where these things can be arranged discreetly.'

'And that would make everything...all right?' she said slowly.

'You won't have any problems, I promise you. Just call me when you know for certain, and we'll do what's necessary. But let's hope for the best. It may be a false alarm.'

Suddenly she couldn't bear the sight of him. Every word he uttered seemed a blow to her heart.

'You'd better leave,' she said. 'Go!'

'Ah, you think he may still turn up? Right. You don't want him to find me here.'

'I didn't say that. I'm not expecting him.'

'Oh, come on! He was good to you. Don't tell me he doesn't want something in return.'

Her eyes blazed. 'Get out before I do something violent.'

He escaped. As the door closed behind him it took all of her self-control not to hurl something at it.

Could he be right? she wondered. Would Travis arrive and demand 'payment', thus proving himself as cynical and self-seeking as every other man?

As the night wore on she tensed at every sound outside her door, waiting for the knock. But it never came, and at last she realised that Travis was better than her fears, better than Lee's spiteful accusations.

Somehow after that it was easier to sleep.

Next morning she rose very early and ordered breakfast through room service. As she was finishing, the phone rang.

'It's me,' said Travis. 'Can I come up or will I be in the way?'

'I'm alone,' she said, correctly interpreting this. 'Do come.'

She was waiting for him with the door open, and shut it quickly behind him.

'I came up the back stairs,' he said. 'Nobody will know I'm here so if Lee…you know…'

'If Lee asks any jealous questions you won't have compromised me,' she said, bitterly amused. 'Don't worry, he won't. And he'd actually be glad you were here.'

'Why would he…? Oh, no, tell me I'm wrong.'

'You'd relieve him of a problem. He was here last night. Not for long. He escaped as soon as he could.'

'You told him about the baby?'

'I told him there might be one. He was horrified. He's probably calling abortion doctors this minute.'

Travis drew in a sharp breath. 'Would you—?'

'No, of course not!' she said passionately. 'Never, *never*! If I'm pregnant I'll have the child, and if its father isn't interested…I'll manage.'

She began to pace the room, clenching and unclenching her hands until he took gentle hold of her.

'Calm down,' he said. 'We've got to find out the truth. We can't do anything until we know one way or the other.'

'You're kind but it's me that's got to do something, not you. I won't drag you into this.'

'I'm already part of this. You "dragged me in" when you socked me on the cheek yesterday.'

'I didn't sock you. It was a light tap and there isn't the slightest mark—'

She stopped. His eyes were full of kindly humour, telling her that he was joking, and she should have realised.

'Just shut up and let me look after you, OK?' he said.

'I don't know what to do next. Perhaps I should go back to England.'

'Before you've established the facts? Surely not.'

'What difference will it make either way if Lee… I don't know… Wait, let me give you this now.'

She took out the expensive necklace he'd loaned her.

'I ought to have given it back to you last night, but there were so many things on my mind—'

'That's all right. I understand.'

'Take it, take it.' She was pushing the necklace into his hands as though desperate to get it out of her possession. It might have been some fearful thing, full of horrific memories, he thought, dismayed.

'All right,' he said, putting the jewels into his pocket. 'Now, let's talk this over calmly.' He drew her to the bed and sat beside her. 'Running away isn't a good idea. I'm not letting you out of my sight until we know what's going to happen. Is there anyone at home for you?'

'No, I live with my grandparents but they're away at the moment.'

'What about other family? Brothers, sisters?'

'Nobody, but that doesn't matter. I'm strong, I can cope. Please don't worry about me.'

He got up and strode to the window, standing with his back to her while he tried to get his head round what was happening. Before him stretched Sunset Boulevard, a glamorous place that seemed to typify the world he took for granted; a world in which presentation was all-important and most things had a price, even if it was often dressed up with tinsel.

Take whatever life offered, give as little as possible in return. That was the conventional wisdom. He'd gained much from Charlene's presence. Now she was obligingly offering to vanish, causing no trouble, asking no favours, even handing back jewellery that many women would have tried to claim. It couldn't be better and a shrewd man would seize what she'd given him, pack her onto the next plane, bless his luck and forget about her.

Travis made a slight turn, glancing over his shoulder at where she still sat on the bed. She wasn't looking at him, just staring blankly into space.

This was how she would cope, he thought; sitting alone in an empty house, looking into the distance. Abandoned by her lover, abandoned by the man who'd called himself her friend and brother.

Common sense demanded that he get rid of her

while she was still doing him good and before she could become awkward.

But common sense had never been his strong suit, he thought wryly. Almost everyone who knew him agreed about that.

'So now we have to get moving,' he said, returning to sit beside her. 'Hurry up and pack.'

His businesslike tone sent a faint chill through her. He was dumping her, and she couldn't blame him. But somehow it wasn't what she'd expected.

But she should have expected it, she thought, depressed. Clearly he was as unreliable as Lee!

She pulled herself together. 'Time I was going.'

'No, you're not,' he said firmly. 'You're coming to stay with me.'

'With you—where?'

'In my apartment. Nobody will know you're there and you'll have privacy as long as you want it. And don't give me any more nonsense about how strong you are because every time you say it I believe it less and less. And if you really think I'm the kind of rotten friend who'd abandon you when you need a hand to hold, well—thanks for the insult.'

'I never meant to insult you. I just didn't want to be a burden. I have no claim on you.'

'Except the claim of gratitude. After last night I owe you big-time. Brenton's flaming mad, which is great. It means he knows he's losing the fight and it's due to you. You're my best defence, and there's no way I'm going to let you leave Los Angeles. I'm taking you prisoner. Get used to it. Do as you're told!'

Without warning, she was flooded by tears. Whatever he said, the truth was that he was protecting her out of kindness. The macho words were just a smokescreen.

'Hey, come on,' he said, taking her into a firm hug. 'No need to cry.'

'I'm not crying,' she wept.

'Of course you're not. You're much too strong for that, aren't you?'

In despair, she shook her head.

'I'm going downstairs,' he told her. 'I'll be back in a moment. Don't even think of locking me out, unless, of course, Lee appears, in which case I'll vanish.'

But that wouldn't happen, and they both knew it.

When he'd gone she packed her things, moving

mechanically. What happened now was beyond her control. She was in Travis's hands, his dependant, even perhaps his victim.

The thought should have troubled her but it didn't. Stronger than anything was the feeling of having landed safely in the middle of a storm.

CHAPTER FIVE

WHEN Travis returned Charlene was ready with everything packed.

'We have to decide on the PR,' he said. 'It's part of living in Los Angeles. PR gets hard-wired into you. You decide what you're actually doing, and then decide what you want the world to think you're doing. They're not usually the same thing.'

'Right,' she said, in the voice of someone trying to hang in there. 'How do we decide?'

'We must consider whether we want to be seen together. Last night we were, and it was great, but your priority is still Lee, so let's be discreet until that situation is sorted. It's best if nobody sees us leave together, so we'll go down the back stairs.'

'But my bill—'

'That's sorted. Just take my hand.'

It felt inevitable to put her hand in his and feel him clasp it in a firm, comforting grip. Looking back afterwards, she had the feeling that this moment had shone a light on the path ahead. From now on she would go where he led.

Quietly they descended, to find Rick waiting halfway down. He seized her suitcase and hurried ahead. By the time they reached the door he was there with the car. Nobody saw them get inside and settle in the back as the car glided out of the hotel's rear car park into Sunset Boulevard.

It was still early in the day and the sun was rising high. Already the street was busy and she looked out at it with fascination.

'I looked it up online before I came out here,' she said in wonder, 'but nothing really prepares you.'

'That's true. I grew up here but it still makes me think—*get down*!'

Next moment he'd seized her, drawing her close so that her head was against his shoulder, everything about him radiating alarm.

'There was someone I knew,' he said from above her head. 'I don't think they saw your face, but let's keep it hidden and not take chances. Sorry to grab you like that. I hope I didn't hurt you.'

'No, I'm fine,' she managed to say.

She could feel one of his hands on her hair while the other lay gently over her face, just enough to conceal her features from anyone who happened to be close.

'Sorry about this,' he said. 'I'll release you as soon as it's safe.'

'Don't worry. I'm quite comfortable.'

She felt him move so that he leaned down over her, concealing his own face as much as possible.

'Get into the back streets as soon as possible, Rick,' he called.

The next moment the car swung wildly around a corner so that she had to move quickly to cling to Travis.

'OK?' he asked.

'Sure. No worries.'

'Charlene,' he said, as he sensed something amazing, *'are you laughing?'*

'I guess I am.' She chuckled. 'Don't ask me why. It's mad, crazy. Whatever I expected, it wasn't this.'

'Me neither,' he admitted. 'But that's life, isn't it?'

'I guess it's more fun that way.'

'Definitely. And at all costs, let life be fun.'

Now he too was laughing, enfolding her in his arms. She felt his body in her hands, against her own body, and she knew a flash of wisdom. It was lucky she was in no danger of falling in love with him, because otherwise this delicious moment could seriously threaten her common sense.

Luckily she was safe. Quite safe.

She repeated that again. Completely safe.

After a while he said, 'I think we could risk it now,' loosening his grip and easing her up from his shoulder.

'I've made a mess of your hair,' he said, brushing it back.

'And of course my hair is what I'm chiefly concerned about.'

'Well, some girls would be,' he said wryly. 'Never mind. When we get home you can spend the day looking after yourself.'

'Where do you live?'

'Beachwood Canyon, part of the Hollywood Hills.'

Soon she could see the land rising steeply above them, crowned by the famous HOLLYWOOD sign that defined this magical place. Much of Hollywood's activities had now drifted to other parts of the city, but this was where it had all begun. Humphrey Bogart had lived here, also

Charlie Chaplin. In this place was enshrined much of the city's glamorous history, especially in the part known as Beachwood Canyon.

As they climbed higher and higher, Charlene gazed out of the window, riveted. Soon they were driving along a street lined with palm trees, until they came in sight of a three-storey block.

'I'm on the top floor,' he said.

His cellphone rang and he answered it impatiently. 'Yes, I'm on my way—something came up—I'll call you back.'

'Am I making you late for work?' she asked anxiously.

'Don't worry about it. I'll show you in and then dash off.'

Luck favoured them in the elevator ride to the top, and they entered his home without being seen.

'I've got to go now,' he said at once. 'The spare bedroom's over there. Make yourself at home. Raid the fridge. The place is yours. Here's my phone number. Call me if anything worries you.'

'I can't call you while you're working,' she said, aghast. 'What would your bosses say?'

'Nothing. The only thing that upsets them is if I damage my public image. But if I behave like a spoilt brat on-set it's just dismissed as part of my "great star" personality.'

The wicked gleam in his eyes robbed the words of conceit. To him it was all a joke, she realised, and if the joke was against himself he enjoyed that best of all.

'We're not filming today, just rehearsing again. So call me if you need to.'

'All right, I'll do whatever you think best.'

'Now that's wisdom talking. And don't worry. Everything's going to be fine.'

He vanished.

Yes, she thought. He could make her feel that all would be well as long as he was there. It was a rare gift.

The apartment was luxurious but in a down-to-earth way that pleasantly surprised her. Instinct told her that the man who lived here wasn't 'full of himself' as he might so easily have become. He just liked his own way. Which was fair enough, she reckoned.

Charlene spent the day as he'd said, making herself at home, eating a snack from the fridge, always alert for a call from Lee. But when the phone rang in the late morning it was Travis to ask how she was. Later he called again to say he was on his way home.

But from Lee, not a word.

When Travis arrived he gave her a searching look and said quietly, 'Nothing?'

'Nothing.'

'He just needs a little time to think about it. Now, let's have supper, if you can stand my cooking.'

He was no chef but his cooking was edible. As they devoured chicken he said, 'Lee kept giving me some odd looks today. He doesn't know whether he's coming or going.'

'I think he'd like to be going,' she said sadly. 'Then he could get away from me.'

'He's probably just confused. He might be a father, or he might not. He needs to know for sure before he can decide how he feels.'

'You talk as if you know,' she said curiously.

'It happened to me once. We'd known each other a while, then she said she was expecting but she didn't know if it was mine or not. In the end we found that it wasn't.'

'Did you mind?' she asked, struck by a new note in his voice.

'It might have been nice. A baby anchors you to reality, tells you where you belong.'

'But you have all those brothers.'

'Yes, but at a distance. I hear about them, and about my father, and it's like getting messages from another universe. If her baby had been mine nothing could have kept me away, and Lee will probably be the same when he knows.'

'Yes,' she said, knowing she didn't sound convinced.

'Are you really in love with him?'

'I don't know. We had that time together—and it was so sweet, so close. I really wanted that closeness.'

'I know the feeling,' he said quietly. 'And at least I had my brothers, even if they lived at a distance. But you have nobody except your grandparents, is that right?'

'I have a stepbrother, James, but we're not in contact. My mother and his father took a trip to celebrate their wedding anniversary, and never came back. Their plane crashed. The last time I saw James was at their funeral.'

'And your grandparents? Are they any comfort to you in this situation?'

'I haven't told them. They know I'm in Los Angeles but not why. If it works out badly I don't want to spoil their African holiday.'

'So you knew it might work out badly,' he said, 'right from the day you came out here?'

'Yes, well—you always hope for the best, don't you?'

'That's right. Keep on hoping.'

Travis squeezed her hand and they sat in silence for a moment.

'What do you think of this place?' he asked at last, rising to fetch more coffee.

'Fascinating. Especially your bookcase. All that Shakespeare.'

'You were naturally surprised to find that a TV actor is bright enough to understand Shakespeare.'

'No, I didn't mean that,' she said hurriedly.

He grinned. 'Didn't you? All right, I'll take your word for it. Actually, the only play I know well is *A Midsummer Night's Dream*. That's how I understood what you were saying about how you met Lee. I acted in it once, years ago.'

'Were you Lysander or Demetrius?' she asked, naming the two young male leads.

'Neither. I played Puck.'

Of course, she thought. Puck, the fiendish but delightful elf, described by one person as a 'shrewd and knavish sprite' and by himself as 'that merry wanderer of the night'. He spent the play performing roguish tricks and laughing at the chaos that resulted.

Strangely, Puck was the perfect role for Travis. His 'romantic hero' looks might seem more suitable for one of the lovers but the sense of delightfully wicked mischief that pervaded him suggested a different story. And something told Charlene that this was his true self.

'I'm just staggered by the window in my room,' she said. 'Enormous. Floor to ceiling. And that long view down to the city. It's the most beautiful thing I've ever seen.'

'The ones in my room are even better,' he said. 'Come and look. It's a sight you'll never forget.'

Taking her hand, he drew her into his room and made a gesture of revelation. Charlene gasped as she saw the two huge breathtaking walls of glass, angled to form a corner. It wasn't yet completely dark, but evening was closing in and the lights of Los Angeles gleamed against the shadows.

'I was wrong before,' she breathed. '*This* is the

most beautiful thing I've ever seen. Nothing else could ever be like it. Oh, goodness!'

'That's how I feel,' Travis agreed. 'I look at the view every night before I go to bed.'

'And the HOLLYWOOD sign,' she said, pointing into the distance. 'Just to remind you what it's all about.'

'All about,' he murmured, his eyes fixed on the view. Briefly he glanced at her over his shoulder. 'Do we ever really know what it's all about?'

'Perhaps it's better not to,' she suggested.

'That could be the wisest thing you've ever said.'

He gazed at the view a moment longer, then pulled the huge curtains closed and led her out of the room.

'An early night for me. After this morning I was warned not to be late again.'

Charlene tidied away plates in the kitchen, then glanced briefly out of a small window that looked out over the front of the building. Suddenly she tensed. Beneath the lamp at the gate she'd just glimpsed a woman followed by a man.

And the woman had red hair.

Pictures raged through her mind. The lap dancer

who'd set her sights on Travis in the club—she had red hair, didn't she?

It was impossible.

Was it?

Like the sound of approaching fate, she heard the elevator rise and come to a halt. The next moment Travis's bell rang.

She flew into the hall as he approached the front door, catching him just as he reached out to open it. By using all her weight, she was just able to stop him.

'Hey, what—?'

'That girl who sat on your lap. She had red hair, didn't she?'

'Yes, but—'

'It's her out there.'

'*What?* Are you sure?'

'I caught a glimpse of her hair as she went under the lamp. Don't you see what they're doing? If you open up, she'll grab you and the photographer will pounce. Frank Brenton warned us that he'd try something else.'

'Then it's time I hit back. Stand aside.'

He made a lunge for the front door. By using all

her strength, she was just able to slam him back against the wall.

'Hey, what are you doing?'

'Stopping you making the biggest mistake of your life. Open that door and you're finished. But you're not going to, because I'm not going to let you.'

'Oh, you're not?'

'No, I'm not.'

'Look, I know you mean well, but it's time for action. I'm going to put a stop to their tricks.'

'But you won't. You'll simply hand them another weapon and there'll be no end to it. Your only hope is to play it cool. Let them hammer on the door as much as they like. It won't open.'

'Won't it?' he growled.

'No, because with your usual brilliance you've seen through their rotten little trick and you're one up on them. That'll teach Frank Brenton. He won't enjoy being made a fool of.'

Travis had been trying to free himself from her, but now he stopped, staring into her face as light dawned.

'It could work,' he said.

'It's *going* to work. Here's what we do. Make sure

all the lights are off and go to bed. When you're in your room don't be tempted to pull open the curtains. You're not there. You're not here. You're not anywhere. And don't answer the phone.'

He gave her a stunned look. 'Remind me never to get on your wrong side.'

'That's a promise.'

The doorbell rang again. She felt Travis tense, and tightened her grip in case he yielded to temptation. But he stayed completely still, seemingly turned to stone while the bell rang and rang.

Then the knocking began. Fists thundered against the door, growing louder when they received no response.

'Let's leave them to it,' Charlene said softly, drawing him away.

'Will they never stop?'

'Probably not. So what? Let them go on all night. If you don't go to the door they'll gain nothing.'

'You think they really would keep that up all night?'

'Unless your neighbours lose patience and threaten them with the police.'

'Think what a story that would make,' Travis mused, beginning to laugh.

'Oh, yes.' She laughed with him and they stood together in the dim hallway, shaking, holding on to each other.

'Hey!' From outside the door came an angry yell. 'Stop that noise. Some of us want to get some sleep.'

Mumbles, arguments, exasperation. Finally silence.

But then came the sound of Travis's cellphone.

'Don't answer it,' Charlene said quickly.

'Don't worry, I'm not going to. I can see it's a number I don't recognise. Take no chances.'

'And you won't answer it if it rings again later?'

'I promise you can safely let me out of your sight. Play it cool. I'm learning a lot from you.'

Another noise from below.

'That sounded like the front door being slammed.' Travis went to the tiny window and peered through the crack. 'Yes, they're going. It's over.'

'Yippee! We beat them.'

'You beat them. I'd have walked right into the trap.' He regarded her with a touch of awe. 'What was that remark about my usual brilliance? Someone was brilliant, but it wasn't me.'

He hugged her, not briefly or lightly, but with both arms folded around her, holding her tight.

'Goodnight,' he said softly. 'Thanks for everything.'

He saw her to her door before going to his own room. There he lay awake for a while, enjoying a feeling of contentment. It was strange to feel that way, he thought, given how recently his nerves had been jangling, but all was well. Instinct, stronger than words, told him that.

Just once he got up and went out into the hall, lingering outside her door, wondering if by chance Lee was calling her. But there was only silence, and after a while he went back to bed. Smiling, he snuggled down and slept the sleep of the innocent.

When they met in the kitchen next morning Travis eyed her with an air of caution.

'Is everything OK?' she asked.

'I'm not sure. I'm becoming nervous of you.' He rubbed his shoulder where it had rammed against the wall in their tussle. 'Women are supposed to be the weaker sex, but I guess that's just a myth.'

'Just beware us when we're really determined.' She laughed.

'I learned that last night.' He rubbed his shoulder again. 'I'm getting used to you beating me up.'

Suddenly he dropped his joking manner.

'But I'm glad you did. You really saved me from disaster. Why I was crazy enough to argue with you—if I'd opened the door—'

'It did seem strange. I thought you were being cautious.'

'I was, but I lost my temper. It doesn't happen often, so when it does I don't tend to think straight.' He touched her face. 'Thank you. Thank you more than I can say.'

She placed her hand over his and held it against her cheek, moved by an emotion for which there were no words.

'I told you about my doctor friend,' he said. 'I'm going to send her to see you. She's a nice lady. She'll do that test, then you'll know and you can make decisions.'

Charlene nodded. 'Yes, that's the best way. Thank you.'

'Don't thank me. I'm in your debt, not the other way around. I'll call you. Bye.'

He kissed her cheek and departed.

Dr Grace Hanley arrived an hour later. She was

in her forties with a mature, kindly face. Charlene tried not to feel too nervous. This was it. The final answer.

They got quickly down to business and soon Grace was studying the test cylinder with a face that revealed nothing.

'Were you hoping to be pregnant?' she asked.

'I'm not sure. Does that mean it's a negative?'

'Yes, I'm afraid so.'

'But at least…now I know. Thank you, Doctor. Can I make you some coffee?'

She was trying to sound normal and untroubled, but the doctor evidently understood her inner turmoil because she declined, patted her hand gently, and departed.

The walls of the apartment seemed to crush Charlene in bleak, hopeless silence. So that was that. It had all been for nothing. She'd made a fool of herself by pursuing a man who didn't want her.

She lay down, trying to control her flickering memories. There was Lee, or was it Demetrius, smiling as they came offstage after a rehearsal, complimenting her.

'Hey, you really played that scene for all it was worth. Wow!'

And herself, dazzled to receive a compliment from such a knowledgeable source, gazing at him, starry-eyed.

She could see him now, warming to her, holding her in his arms, smiling as they made love.

Or was it love? Perhaps on her side, but whatever he'd been making it wasn't love. She should have faced that earlier.

Yet if there had been a baby, might his feelings not have warmed, flowering into family affection that would embrace her and their child?

Instead—nothing.

Nothing!

She was seized by a fierce longing for Travis to be there, wrapping her in his arms, offering brotherly comfort that would have made this bearable.

No!

The ferocity of her emotion made her sit up. Hell would freeze over before she became a pathetic, needy creature, clinging to Travis. He would be kind, she knew, but soon the kindness would become forced, as he strove to conceal his exasperation.

That mustn't happen. The moment she sensed him thinking, *How long must I put up with this?*

was the moment she would inwardly die. Or run a mile. Or both.

When he came home she was waiting for him, calm and smiling.

'Everything all right?' he asked.

'Everything's fine.'

He didn't ask her for the test result. It would have been dishonest when he already knew. As promised, Grace had discreetly texted him one word: *No.* It might be a disgraceful violation of professional confidence, but friends did that for each other. So he waited for Charlene to speak, which at last she did.

'I'm not pregnant, so that's that.' She made a gesture of finality. 'I'll make some coffee.'

She turned away but he detained her. 'Wait a moment. "That's that"? Nothing more? You don't care?'

'Not really. This always seemed likely. And besides, something else has happened.' She laid her hand over her stomach.

'You mean you've finally—?'

'Yes. I don't know what made me late in the first place, but perhaps it was caused by tension because it started barely an hour after the doctor left. Anyway, it's the clincher. There's no baby. There never was, thank goodness.'

Her voice was bright and efficient, informing him that all was well.

But he didn't believe it. All was far from well with a woman who could wear such a dead smile.

'Well, I can see it solves one problem,' he said cautiously.

'It solves all the problems. Think of the catastrophe if I'd been pregnant while Lee… *Ugh!*' She shivered. 'It doesn't bear thinking about.'

Travis was troubled by an inner desire, as mysterious as it was illogical, to hear that she was saddened by the news. But she was bright, breezy, practical. And she froze his heart.

In the kitchen she made coffee, talking without stopping.

'I'm really sorry to have given you all this trouble. Just think of me making so much fuss about nothing. You must be good 'n' mad.'

'Not at all,' he said in an equally unrevealing voice. 'These things happen. You have to deal with matters as they come up. Sooner or later we all of us—'

Stop burbling, Travis told himself in disgust.

'I hope you don't mind but I have to vanish,' he told her. 'I've got a lot of lines to learn. Goodnight.'

He grabbed a sandwich and fled to his room.

So all was well. A potentially awkward situation had vanished. He could continue on his way, planning, calculating, arranging things for his own benefit, doing everything with an eye on his career.

It was absurd to be disappointed at her sensible reaction. What had he expected?

As the light failed he rose and drew the curtains across the great windows, shutting out the view. Just to the side was Charlene's window, already almost covered by curtain, with just a gap of a few inches left.

There she was, a shadow standing in the gap. Her light was off and in the near darkness it was hard to discern her. He switched off his own light so that he could watch, unobserved in the darkness.

She stood quite still, looking down at Los Angeles, then gazing up into the sky. Now he could see her face a little more clearly. It was sad, and there was a hint of tears on her cheeks. The mask had fallen away, revealing loneliness and despair.

Then she did something that broke his heart, leaning her head against the glass, clasping her arms about her body as though to protect herself from some unknown danger, and rocking back and forth.

That was the truth, he thought, cursing himself for stupidity. And she didn't trust him enough to let him see her grief. How had he been so easily fooled?

For a few minutes he paced the floor, then walked out into the hall, heading for her room. But at her door he stopped, aghast at what he could hear from the other side.

'What's the next flight to London?' came Charlene's voice. 'Midday tomorrow? Right, I'd like to book a ticket—'

The crash of her door being thrown open made her look up. '*Hey, what are you doing?* Give me that phone.'

'Like hell!' Travis said, shutting it down. 'What do you think *you're* doing?'

'Booking my flight home.'

'And no thought for anyone else,' he raged. 'Who cares about the damage you'll do to me? I put my neck on the line for you, Charlene. I've done everything I could to help you. And this is how you thank me. People saw us together, it gave them ideas. Just how do you think I'll look if they know you've fled the country without a backward glance? They'll laugh themselves sick. I can just hear them—*Guess he must be losing his touch! Ho, ho, ho!*

'I didn't make an issue of this when Lee was still in the picture, but now it's different. You can rescue me or make a fool of me, and you didn't give me a thought.'

'Travis, please, I didn't realise—'

'No, you didn't. I still have problems about that lap dancer. Brenton isn't giving up, and you're the only person who can help. So what do you do? Abandon me.'

'I'm sorry. You're right; I do owe you some help.'

'Yes, I think you do, but of course if you don't want to bother—' he retorted.

'I do, I do! I just didn't think—I'm really sorry—tell me what to do.'

'I want you to stay here, in this apartment. Let the world think we're a couple.'

'But will that help your image? If people believe we're living together—is that respectable?'

'It is these days. At one time it would have been a scandal, but now a lot of unmarried couples share a home, and as long as they're faithful to each other nobody thinks anything of it. It's lap dancers that get you into trouble. While you're here, you're my protection against Brenton and his nasty tricks.'

'All right; you give the orders.'

'That's what I like to hear.'

She was baffling, he thought. Nobody, seeing her now, could have suspected the agonised despair that had consumed her only a few minutes ago. She must be a better actress than he'd realised.

But then, his own performance had been admirable. Outraged pride, indignation at her 'ingratitude'; these had been master strokes born of desperation. When he'd thought of her returning to England to sit alone in an empty house, he'd known that he had to stop her at all costs. So he'd assumed a new character, aggressive, self-centred, as different from the real Travis as it was possible to get.

If he said it himself, it had been an award-winner of a performance.

At her bedroom door he said, 'You'll still be here tomorrow?'

'Word of honour.'

'Goodnight. Sleep tight.'

He walked away without even the briefest backward glance. It took a lot of self-control, but he was getting good at that.

CHAPTER SIX

AT BREAKFAST next day Travis said, 'Has Lee called you?'

'No.'

Nor would he, Travis thought. He'd dive for cover and hope the storm would pass.

'Have you called him?' he asked.

'No.'

'You can't put it off for ever.' He added reluctantly, 'Would you like me to—?'

'Thanks, but no. There are some things I must do for myself.' Charlene gave a little laugh. 'Oh, Travis, if you could see your face. I've never seen a man so relieved.'

'Yes,' he admitted. 'But I'd have done it if you'd really wanted me to.'

How kind he was! she thought. How different from anyone else! Impulsively, she laid a fond hand on his cheek, and he put his own hand over it.

'Time to make our plans,' he said. 'I need to flaunt you a bit. I hope you don't mind.'

'Not at all.'

'We must announce ourselves to the world as a couple. An evening out together, in the spotlight, should do it. The Stollway Hotel is best because they already know you there.'

'Fine. What about the "stage directions"? You'll have to give me detailed instructions.'

'Good idea. Do you remember, when you go into the hotel there's a broad staircase leading up from Reception to a landing with a huge picture? Go up there to admire the picture. Stay there until I arrive.'

'And while you're looking for me you must turn around slowly a few times,' she said, 'so everyone can get a good view of you.'

'Right. Walk down the stairs very slowly. I'll be waiting at the bottom, looking up at you, riveted with admiration. Or should it be adoration?'

'Hmm, I don't think so,' she said, considering this seriously. 'Admiration will be enough for now. Adoration can come later.'

'Aren't I allowed to fall ecstatically at your feet, overcome with worship?'

'Not just yet, I think.'

'Very well, I'll control my ardour—for the moment. Later I'll turn up the heat and sigh yearningly at my goddess. Hey, do you mind? Women don't usually burst out laughing when I say things like that.'

'They would if they could listen to you now,' she choked, struggling to get her mirth under control. 'And just how often do you say "things like that"?'

'Let's leave it,' he said hastily. 'I'm glad you find it so funny.'

'You're not glad at all,' she teased.

He ground his teeth. 'Have you finished?'

'Yes.'

'Then I'll continue. You come down the stairs and when you reach me I'll take your hand and draw you close. With any luck, somebody will have a cellphone with a camera, so we'll give them a sight to enjoy.'

'What will you be wearing?'

'Dinner jacket and bow tie. What about you? I think you'll need a new wardrobe while you're here, which gives us a bit of a problem.'

'What kind of a problem?'

'Since you're doing this for me, it's my responsibility to pay for the new clothes. But if I offer I suppose you'll come over all offended, and if our last meetings are anything to go by you'll thump the living daylights out of me. Ah, well, I guess I'll just have to get used to it. Here.' He pushed a credit card across the table.

'Go to—' He named a famous purveyor of fashionable clothes for both men and women. 'I'll call them and say you have my permission to use that. Get a whole wardrobe.'

'Just the dress for tonight. Restrained and *respectable*! They'll take one look and know that you've opted for a life of virtue.' She eyed him satirically. 'However unlikely that might seem!'

He grinned. 'I refuse to answer on the grounds that it may incriminate me.' He checked his watch. 'Hey, I've got to be going. I'm being interviewed by a journalist.'

'What will you tell them?'

'Nothing much. Just drop a few mysterious hints. Get them wondering. That's far more effective.'

'You really know how to make people dance to your tune, don't you? I suppose that's as big a talent as acting.'

'Yes, and I'm not the only one who has it,' he said, regarding her significantly.

Wanting to do him proud, Charlene concentrated fiercely on getting her appearance right for that evening. The gown she chose was dark red velvet with a neckline that came modestly up to the base of her throat, but which hugged her slender figure temptingly. She reckoned that was a good compromise.

She was pleased, too, with the way the hairdresser swept up her hair in an exquisite display of elegance, leaving just a few long curls drifting down over her neck.

It was important to be always ready to embrace new experiences. Tonight she was going to dine with the handsomest, most charming man she'd ever met, revelling in the attention he would pay her and the envy of other women. And that was quite definitely a new experience.

'Time for curtain up!' she murmured. 'Let the performance begin.'

At the agreed time, Travis entered the hotel lobby. There was an immediate rustle of interest as he went to stand at the foot of the stairs as she descended slowly, her eyes fixed on him, as his were on her. In a white tuxedo and bow tie, he was at his starry best.

If I was a dreamy teenager, she thought, amused, *I could fall for him. Lucky for both of us that I'm not.*

Following the stage directions, he reached out and took her hand, murmuring, 'Charlene.' Then he brushed his lips against her fingers, whispering her name again.

'Travis.' She sighed.

Holding her head high, she allowed him to draw her across the floor to the restaurant. A waiter showed them to the table and was about to pull out her chair when Travis stopped him, indicating that he alone would perform this service for his lady. Only when he was certain that she was at ease did he attend to his own comfort.

When the wine waiter appeared he asked her tenderly, 'Do you have a preference…my darling?'

'I'll let you choose.' She sighed.

He gave an order, adding, 'And a bottle of your very best champagne.' Leaning towards Charlene, he added, 'We need to celebrate.'

The waiter eyed them with new interest, ears

alert for Charlene's reply. 'Isn't it a little soon to celebrate?' she asked.

'Not for us,' Travis assured her. When the waiter was out of earshot he murmured, 'That got him.'

'You're just a natural-born deceiver,' she murmured back.

'Thank you for the compliment. Of course I am. It's what acting's all about. He who deceives best gets top billing.'

'And the best pay?'

'Naturally. A wise old actor once told me, "When the crowds are cheering, the applause is deafening and they're fighting to hire you, never forget that you could be out of work tomorrow." And he was right.'

Which was why, she thought, he was so determined to protect what he had, using any method necessary.

The food was served. It was excellent, and they both tucked in with pleasure. As he ate, Travis was studying her appearance with approval.

'Superb,' he said. 'Modest but attractive. Give my congratulations to the wardrobe mistress.'

When they had finished eating and were alone again, Travis said, 'I think this is the right moment.'

'Right moment for what?'

'I stopped in a jeweller's shop and bought you a small gift.'

'That sounds like it would fit the script,' she said, nodding wisely.

'I thought so too.'

From his pocket he took a tiny box that looked as though it might have come from a jeweller's.

'This is for you, my darling,' he said fervently.

Earrings? she wondered. Or a bracelet?

She lingered to give him a dramatic smile of gratitude before opening the box.

Then she stared.

They were certainly earrings, but not diamonds, pearls or anything romantic. They depicted a cartoon character called Daft Doody, very popular with children just then.

'What is it?' he asked, seeing her astonished face. 'Don't you—? Oh, goodness, no! Put it away. It's the wrong box. How did I—?'

His self-reproach was drowned by a burst of laughter from Charlene.

'I'm sorry,' she choked, 'but you must admit it's hilarious.'

'Must I? These are a birthday gift for the little daughter of a friend who's very keen on Daft Doody. I bought them at the same time as your pearl earrings—the boxes are alike and I picked up the wrong one—*hell*!'

'I guess that wasn't in the script,' she said, still chuckling.

He opened his mouth to reply, but then gave up and grinned sheepishly.

'But I don't have your present with me. I brought this one and left yours behind.'

'Don't worry. Actually, I rather like these kiddy earrings. I think I'll keep them. It's all right, don't look like that. Here you are.'

'Thank you,' he groaned, taking the box from her. 'I'll give you yours when we get home.'

'No, no,' she said urgently. 'You can't give them to me privately. What would you gain by that?'

'Right. I'll present them next time we're out.'

'Unless you get confused and bring me a set of cufflinks instead,' she teased.

'I suppose I deserved that.'

'Hey, come on, it's not a tragedy.'

'No, but it's reality. That's the trouble with the life I live. You kind of lose touch with reality until it socks you on the jaw. This is the sort of careless mistake I make easily, and I get away with it because I'm surrounded by people whose job it is to tell me that everything's fine, I'm doing well.'

'They just want to boost your confidence so that you can give your all to the performance.'

'I know, but it can be dangerous if you hear it too often. You get conceited, start thinking that whatever you do is perfect, but in real life it isn't and you make an idiot of yourself.'

She was intrigued. Travis had opened a small window, allowing her a glimpse of the confusions and complications deep inside him. She would have sought to know more but, as though suddenly alerted to danger, he closed the window and resumed a cheerful manner, raising his champagne glass.

'What are we celebrating?' she asked.

'You! Your genius and daring.'

She lifted her glass and they saluted each other.

'This is going to be fun,' he said. 'Here's to fraud, cheating and dishonesty.'

'What would life be without them?'

Charlene leaned back in her chair, taking a faintly incredulous look around the luxurious restaurant, trying to believe she was really here.

'What are you thinking?' he asked.

'I'm just surprised that I'm enjoying myself so much after all that's happened. It's so nice to sit and talk, and say what you really mean.'

He nodded. 'Yes, I find it's a rare pleasure too.'

'Talking to you is like having that big brother I dreamed of. Oh!' She covered her mouth with her hand as though concealing a guilty secret. 'No, sorry! I shouldn't have said that.'

'Said what?'

She gave a quick glance over her shoulder to make sure nobody was listening, then mouthed, 'Brother!'

'Ah, yes! I see. Brother's not the image we're trying to convey to the world, is it?' He assumed a tone of mock severity. 'Be more careful next time.'

She gave a brief salute. 'Aye, aye, sir!'

They laughed and he said warmly, 'But in private, brother and sister is ideal.'

'Right. Friends, allies, siblings.'

They shook on it.

She regarded him fondly, saying, 'And you'll always know that you're safe with me.'

'Safe in what sense? Safe because you're not

going to knock me out, kick my shins, poison my coffee?'

'That too. But safe chiefly because I'm not going to lose my heart to you. I promise faithfully! You're not my type.'

'Hmm!' He frowned with comical emphasis. 'That's not what I'm used to hearing.'

'I know. You're used to females who swoon and yearn and say you're the handsomest man in the world. Sorry. No can do! But think how much you'll enjoy that. What a relaxing change it'll be!'

'Yes,' he said. 'I suppose it will. Perhaps it's time we were going.'

Charlene spent the next day on a shopping binge, justifying it with the need to acquire suitable costumes for the role she had to play. At last she returned home and collapsed flat out on the bed. Self-indulgence could be exhausting.

Travis called, apologising that something had come up and he wouldn't be home until late. She assured him that all was well, and he hung up hastily, leaving her wondering if the whole arrangement was about to come to an end. Perhaps she'd already served her purpose and was being cast off.

That would be sad. Not because her heart was engaged, for it wasn't. But Travis appealed to her as a nice man: sweet-natured, generous and not corrupted by his fame. If he turned out to be as cynically self-seeking as other men it would be a disappointment.

By chance one of the television channels was showing a whole evening of *The Man From Heaven*. Episodes from the first series were repeated, end to end, and she came to understand Dr Brad Harrison as never before.

Wearing a white coat and a calm expression, he strode through the corridors of Mercyland Hospital. Everyone revered him. His sweet smile calmed their fears. He achieved miraculous medical cures, but more miraculous still were the cures of the heart that followed his tender advice.

Her last view of him was gazing up into the sky, crying, 'That's what we must all remember. Seize the moment whenever it comes. Don't let the chance slip away, or we may regret it for ever.'

His face was illuminated with a mysterious smile. The camera panned away from him, the credits came up. It was over.

'Too handsome and perfect to be true,' she

mused. 'But then, he isn't supposed to be true. He's a glorious fantasy. I pity any girl who forgets that.'

At eleven o'clock he telephoned, full of excitement.

'I need you to come to the studio tomorrow,' he said. 'There are a lot of people anxious to meet you. Lee will be there. Are you all right about meeting him?'

'I've got to see him some time,' she said. 'Let's do it.'

'Right, I'll set it up. Don't wait up. In the meantime, check out "Notes For You".'

This was a website made up of items taken mostly from the cellphones of private individuals, snapping what they saw in the street or in restaurants. Accessing it on her laptop, Charlene wasn't really surprised to discover shots of herself and Travis in the restaurant the previous evening.

'They didn't waste any time,' she murmured. 'But that's what we wanted when we flaunted ourselves.'

She studied herself on the screen. The picture was slightly blurred, but she reckoned that was an advantage.

'A definite improvement,' she decided. 'Elegant

and not *too* dowdy. Let's just hope nobody gets a sharper lens.'

She wondered what was keeping Travis out so late. Work? Or was he 'enjoying himself' in a way that a kind sister would not ask about?

None of her business.

By the time he came in she'd already retired for the night. She heard him close the door of his bedroom, and after that she could go to sleep.

For her appearance at the studio next morning she chose a plain dress and jacket, but let her hair hang about her shoulders to soften the effect. Travis nodded approval. They spoke little on the journey, mindful that the driver could hear everything, but as they walked into the studio she said, 'I looked up "Notes For You". What a start we've made!'

'You're doing a terrific job,' he said. 'I'm grateful. Look, there's an audience waiting.'

The entrance was crowded with people who'd found an excuse to be there when Travis arrived.

'You're a star,' he murmured.

'Help!' she squeaked.

His hand was around her waist, holding her

close. 'Don't worry. Everything will be fine. This guy approaching is Vince, the director.'

Vince was about forty, vigorous, calculating but amiable. He looked Charlene over quickly and seemed pleased.

'Glad to meet a lady I've heard so much about. Travis says you're his guest of honour, so we'll have to make sure you enjoy your visit.'

The day that followed was breathtaking. One by one, all the big shots came to greet her, size her up and nod their approval. It was clear that they had guessed the true situation, since Travis had been seen with her so soon after the scandal. Denzil Raines went so far as to give him the thumbs up and say, 'Well done. Good move.'

Since she was protecting the studio's most valuable property, she was assigned an 'assistant'. This was Vera, a backroom girl who shadowed Charlene with instructions to take care of her needs. At lunchtime Travis took her to the studio cafe.

'Sorry to have left you alone last night,' he said.

'Actually, I wasn't alone. One of the TV channels showed wall-to-wall episodes, and there you were, all the time.'

'You mean you couldn't get rid of me.' He laughed.

'Let's say it was useful for research. I noted the way you end every episode with some declaration about life.' She struck an attitude and recited, '"Seize the moment whenever it comes. Don't let the chance slip away, or we may regret it for ever." Why, what's the matter?'

Travis had groaned and covered his eyes.

'You couldn't have picked a worse example.' He sighed. 'Life imitating art and making a mess of it. I told you about going to the wedding of my brother Darius. While I was there they showed that episode, where I announced "Seize the moment". Unfortunately, my brother Marcel saw it, and it gave him a mad idea. At the reception he announced his engagement to *his* lady love, Cassie.'

'Why is that unfortunate?'

'Because he overlooked the little matter of asking her first.'

'Ouch!'

'Exactly!'

'Did she refuse him in front of everyone?'

'No, she played along in public but refused him

when they were alone. I gather they've now separated.'

'But that's his fault, not yours.'

'I know, but it's depressing. I want to do my family good, not harm them, even indirectly. I'd like to get closer to them. I know we're in different countries but even so—'

'You can be emotionally close even from different countries,' she agreed.

'Yes, we might if things were better, but something always goes wrong. Darius's wedding was the first family celebration I'd managed to get to for ages. I had visions of a friendly reunion with my father. How stupid can you get?'

'Wouldn't he speak to you?'

'He wasn't there. He didn't want Darius to marry Harriet and did all he could to split them up. When he didn't succeed, he was furious and snubbed the wedding.'

'But you're all grown men. Who does he think he is?'

'One of those Roman emperors we were talking about. Probably Nero.'

'I promise never to tell him you said that.'

'Thanks, though I doubt you'll get the chance.'

There it was again, the hint of wry sadness beneath the cheerful mask. But it was gone in a moment. Something across the room had attracted his attention.

'Lee's here,' he said. 'In the doorway, watching us. But don't look round.'

'I wasn't going to. I don't want him to think I'm yearning after him. I must talk to him once, tell him he's got nothing to worry about—' She gave an ironical smile which made Travis put his hand over hers. 'When I've done that we'll draw a line under it and go our different ways, with no looking back.'

'Isn't there always some looking back?' he asked gently.

'A little, but we don't have to be sentimental. What's done is done.'

'That's very good. I just hope you can go on feeling like that. Yearning and regret for what can't be changed can waste your life. Now, I have to go; they're beckoning me.'

Left alone, she brooded. Travis's remarks about the wisdom of not indulging in regrets made her remember his absence the night before. Was he already looking ahead to the day when she would be surplus to his requirements? She guessed he wouldn't cruelly dump her. He would hand her gently into the arms of another suitor, thus preserving her feelings and her dignity.

She supposed she ought to be grateful to him. She couldn't imagine why she wasn't.

'Can I sit down?'

Looking up, she saw Lee, smiling at her in a way that had once made her heart turn over.

'Sure,' she said.

'I've been waiting for the chance, but I didn't want to disturb you when you were with the great man.'

'I tried to call you this morning but your phone was switched off.'

'Yes, it still isn't working properly,' he said with an uneasy laugh.

Suddenly she pitied him. Maybe it wasn't entirely his fault that he was a coward. Not every man could be brave and generous like Travis.

'Stop worrying,' she said. 'It was a false alarm.'

'You mean you're not—?'

'No, I'm not. It's over. *Finito. Kaput.* Nothing for you to worry about.'

He beamed. 'Oh, wow! That's wonderful. Then everything's all right.'

'I suppose if you look at it one way, yes.' It annoyed her that it didn't seem to cross his mind that she might be disappointed. She wondered if anyone else's feelings had ever crossed his mind in his entire life.

'You're quite sure, aren't you?' he asked anxiously. 'There's no chance of a mistake?'

'No chance at all. Stop worrying.'

His whole being was brilliant with joy. 'This is so wonderful.' He leaned forward, seized her face between his hands and planted a smacking kiss on her mouth. 'Bless you for being a great girl!'

He danced away. Charlene stared after him, confused. Where was the devastation she should be feeling? Where was the disappointed love?

Love! said a scathing voice in her mind. *Is that what you called it? More fool you!*

She'd longed to believe it was love, especially when she'd thought she was to have his child. But the bleak emptiness showed her a cruel truth. Her 'love' had been as much an illusion as his; a fantasy created by a lonely girl who yearned for a feeling of belonging.

There was even an incredible sense of relief that nothing now tied her to this irresponsible boy. She was free. Alone, but free.

'Charlene, for pity's sake, what's the matter?'

Travis suddenly appeared in the seat beside her, seizing her, anxiously searching her face.

'You look so strange,' he said frantically. 'I came back for a moment, and when I saw him kiss you I thought…I don't know what I thought. But please, tell me you're all right.'

'I'm fine, thank you,' she said lightly. 'He kissed me from relief, that's all. He's got what he wanted.'

'What about what you want? Did he ever think of that?' he demanded, unconsciously echoing her own thoughts.

'That would only have confused him.'

'Do you want me to punch him?'

She shrugged. 'Whatever for? Everyone's happy.'

'Are they? *Are they?*' His eyes, fixed on hers, were angry and dark with meaning.

She was saved from having to answer by the arrival of Vera, offering to take Charlene to see some more of the studio.

'That sounds great,' Charlene said cheerfully. 'Let's go.'

Her mind seemed to have slipped into another dimension and she enjoyed the tour, especially the last part, where they crept into the rehearsal room just as Travis was confronting Lee in a scene.

'It's best to think a little before you speak,' 'Dr Harrison' was saying. 'Your patients will appreciate it.'

'I do try,' Lee was saying in character. 'But things can get very difficult.'

'Hey, what happened there?' called Vince. 'Travis, you're supposed to simply stand there and look at him, not reach out as though you meant to hit him.'

'Sorry,' Travis said in a tight voice. 'Something made me jump.'

'OK, do it again,' Vince called. 'Travis, remember you're full of warm feeling and generosity.'

'Yeah, right!'

'Let's leave them to it,' Vera murmured, and they slipped away.

Charlene recalled Travis saying he rarely lost his temper and found it hard to cope when he did. But surely he hadn't lost his temper with Lee?

Yet the look on his face had surprised her, and

possibly everyone else in the room. Anger coming out of nowhere.

At the end of the day she went out to wait for him in the car. There were nods and salutations from the others who were leaving, always with an edge of curiosity and respect.

I could get used to this, she thought. *OK, so it's all a con, but who says I can't enjoy a con while it lasts?*

After a few minutes Travis joined her and they relaxed in the back together.

'Do you ever have to drive yourself?' she asked.

'I'm not *allowed* to drive myself,' he said, grinning. 'The bosses say they want me free to think of nothing but my "art". The truth is that I'm not a brilliant driver and they're terrified I'll have an accident that will reflect badly on the show.'

As the car pulled away, Charlene saw Lee watching her from a distance. He waved and quickly stepped back into the shadows. She glanced at Travis, wondering if he'd noticed, but he was looking the other way.

CHAPTER SEVEN

THEY got out a few blocks from his home, and went to dine in a small restaurant.

As they relaxed over the main course, Charlene said, 'We need to talk about money. You give me too much.'

'You deserve every penny. I want you to take more and equip yourself with more clothes.'

'Then I'll buy them myself.'

'At LA prices? No way.'

'I mean it. I'm your useful piece of stage equipment, not your kept woman. This is an arrangement of equals or it's nothing.'

'Equals?' He looked comically alarmed. 'I don't do equals.'

'You've never heard of women's lib?'

'I've heard of it but I try to ignore it. I don't know! My girlfriend paying for herself. Whatever is the world coming to? Well, at least you have to accept this.'

From his pocket he produced a small jewel box. Inside she found the pearl earrings that he'd left behind on the first night.

'Sorry about that,' he said.

'And the press thinks you're the great romantic,' she teased.

He fixed the earrings for her. She had to admit they were beautiful. He thought so too, from the way he was smiling.

They strolled home, yawning, for it was very late. As they got into the elevator a middle-aged man appeared, hurrying. Travis held the doors open for him, calling, 'It's all right, Sam, I've got it.'

'Thanks,' said the man. He smiled and nodded at Charlene.

'Charlene, this is my friend, Sam Barton. He and his wife live on the floor below us.'

'And you don't have to tell me who this is,' Sam said, shaking her hand. 'You're the talk of LA.'

The three of them exchanged pleasantries until the elevator stopped, and Sam bid them goodnight, departing with a curious look at Charlene.

'Nice guy,' Travis said as they finished the journey. 'We must have him and his wife to supper. You'll like Rita.'

'Are they in the business?' Charlene asked. She had fallen easily into the habit of referring to the entertainment world as 'the business' as though there was no other. In Los Angeles it was easy to believe that was true.

'In a way. He works in one of the studios, on the financial side. She used to be a model and a dancer.'

In her own room she prepared for bed, then went to stand by the window and look down on the gleaming city. Just below, she could see the garden, and Travis, sitting there. He was leaning back against a tree, his eyes closed, his lips moving.

It would be fascinating, she thought, to be a bird in the nearby bush, and hear what he was saying. But she doubted she would ever understand him. Today he'd puzzled her afresh—calm, agitated, unpredictable, but never less than the kind man she valued so dearly.

She drew the curtain and stepped back.

Down below, Travis opened his eyes, glancing up to the top of the building. Again he murmured the words that had struck a nerve.

'"Useful piece of stage equipment." Well, I've been warned.'

* * *

They settled into a comfortable pattern, treating each other with the cheerful friendliness of siblings. At her suggestion, he began calling her Charlie.

'She's the real me, sensible and practical. Charlene is the fantasy version.'

He nodded. 'Very clever.'

He had to be away for a few days, shooting outdoor scenes. Every night he called to ask how she was, and she reassured him. Neither of them ever mentioned Lee.

She was glad of a few free days free. It gave her some time alone, which she felt she needed. Now everything about her had changed. Heads turned in the street, people nudged as she went past. If she'd needed confirmation of Travis's fame, she was getting it.

Now some of it seemed to have rubbed off on her. Cameras appeared, voices called, 'Look this way.' She obliged, careful to look pleasant, but always escaped quickly.

'And they keep asking me to give them a quote,' she told him. 'I don't, of course, but they're getting pressing.'

'I'm sorry you're having a hard time.'

'I didn't say I was having a hard time.' She laughed. 'It's got its funny side, but I don't want to risk saying the wrong thing.'

'We'll sort it out, I promise. We need to arrange things so that they come out the way we want. I'll be home soon. I had hoped it might be tonight, but there's been a big delay. I'll see you tomorrow.'

In fact the delay was cleared up sooner than expected, and he managed to make it home at three in the morning. The apartment was dark and he entered quietly.

But as he crossed the hall he heard a burst of laughter from Charlene's room. He wondered what could make a woman shriek with laughter at this hour, and didn't like any of the answers he came up with.

The gentlemanly thing might have been to creep away, without asking questions about something that was none of his business. But he wasn't feeling like a gentleman. If that was Lee, and he had a horrible feeling that it was, then the silly girl must be protected.

Then came her voice again.

'Oh, come on, you can't do that. No, really, you mustn't. Behave yourself!'

Travis didn't hesitate. In a flash he had the door open, seeking Charlene and whoever she was entertaining. But then he stopped on the threshold, taken aback by what met his eyes.

She was alone in the room, sitting at the dressing table, talking into a cellphone. She glanced up at him, and said, 'Travis has just walked in.' She looked up at him. 'It's my grandparents.'

'Your—?'

'I told you about them. They called me from Nairobi and I've been telling them all about you. Hello—Emma, yes, he's still here. You can talk to him.' She handed him the phone.

Even far away in Nairobi they had heard the news from Los Angeles and wanted to thank him for befriending her. Charlene switched the phone onto 'hands free' so that she could hear their voices and join in, and they all spent a very jolly ten minutes.

Afterwards he sat on the edge of the bed, trying to pull himself together.

'You look absolutely knocked out,' she said sympathetically. 'Can I get you something?'

'No, I'll go straight to bed, thank you. I just need to get some sleep and…goodnight.'

He got out, fast.

* * *

Over breakfast next morning he said, 'You really scared me last night, telling someone to stop what they were doing. I thought a man had broken in.'

'No, it was just Frank and Emma. It's incredible, at their age they're such a pair of clowns.'

'Yes, they sounded like good fun,' he agreed. 'I'll hope to meet them some day. When are they coming back?'

'Not for six weeks.'

'But you're not in a rush to leave me, are you?'

'No, I like it here, if it's all right with you.'

'It's a deal then.'

They shook hands and spent the rest of the meal making domestic arrangements. Travis had a cleaner who came in three times a week, but apart from that he managed for himself. When it came to food, he either ate on the way home, arranged a takeout or made himself a basic snack. Charlene made a list of his favourite meals, studied it and set herself to practise seriously.

'You're a great cook,' he said a week later. 'You get better every day.'

'I do my best.'

'Then congratulations. It's a fantastic best.'

'And there's something else.' She took out a large

envelope, filled with pieces of paper. 'I found this by accident. It just fell out and I had to gather up the papers from the floor.'

He groaned. 'They're receipts I'm supposed to send to my accountant. I'm afraid I let them get into a mess.'

'I can see that. And where you've made notes and done sums—well, never mind. I've been through, trying to put them in some sort of order.'

She handed him the list she'd made, and his face brightened.

'Hey, they actually make sense. I could send this to my accountant without a load of apologies. That's great!'

'So you don't mind? You don't feel I violated your privacy?'

'Charlie, you can violate my privacy any time you like,' he said fervently. 'In fact there are several things—'

In a short time she was privy to all his financial details, including investments. His accountant was a big name but there were a hundred smaller matters that Travis needed to get organised before sending them to him. And among his many talents efficiency and good order found no place.

With delight he dumped everything on Charlene. Now she had access to all his computer accounts, including passwords, enabling her to access his bank account every morning. This she did, several times raising queries, one of which averted a minor disaster.

Travis rewarded her with a glittering gold pendant, but what really pleased her was his look of joy and relief, and his exclamation, 'However did I manage without you?'

'Your own private bank clerk!' She chuckled.

'Bank clerk,' he said softly. 'Is that what you call it?'

Both his eyes and his voice told her that he called it something entirely different. But just what that something might be he wasn't ready to say.

Charlene enjoyed life in Beachwood Canyon. Despite its glamorous location, it closely resembled a village, with a coffee shop, a market and a number of little boutiques where people could meet casually. She saw several faces that she recognised, famous actors and musicians. At first she was tempted to stare, then realised that she too was being stared at.

'How are you coping?' asked an elderly man

who came to sit beside her in a coffee shop. After a moment she recognised him as a once famous star, known for his dynamic sexiness, but now in his eighties.

'It is you, isn't it?' she asked.

'Yes, it's me. I'm flattered to be remembered.'

'I saw you on television in…you know, the film that nearly won you the Best Actor award.'

'The operative word being "nearly". In those days they were practically the only awards. These days there's a whole host of them, especially for TV shows. The TopGo Television Drama Awards are coming up soon and they say your guy's going to scoop every prize going. There's five categories he can be nominated for and the big money says he'll win every one. You two will have a great time at the award ceremony.'

'If I'm still here.'

'Sure you'll be here. Everyone says he's crazy about you. Are you saying he isn't?'

'I'm saying it's private.' She chuckled.

'Good for you. If I hadn't given so many interviews about things that should have stayed private I'd still be married to my second wife, or perhaps my third.'

They settled into a happy discussion, after which Charlene finished the day with a visit to a boutique that was as fashionable as anything to be found in the city. By now she was a little short of time, but she had her eye on a pair of stretch jeans.

'The size looks about right for me,' she said. 'You close in five minutes, don't you? I'll take them.'

Back in the apartment, she pulled on the jeans and considered herself thoughtfully.

They're just a little tighter than I thought, she mused. *Too tight? Yes? No? If my rear was bigger I could be accused of flaunting it, but I'm so skinny I can get away with it.*

But 'skinny' wasn't the right word, she knew. While not voluptuous, her behind was nicely shaped, elegantly curved.

She found a floaty chiffon blouse that hung loosely down over the revealing trousers, concealing her rear from general sight.

From the front door came the sound of a knock and a cry, 'Is anyone there?'

'Coming,' she called.

Outside, she found a middle-aged woman with a tall, lithe figure.

'Hello,' she said. 'I'm Rita Barton, your neighbour from the next floor down. I came to return something I borrowed from Travis.'

She had a bright, cheerful face and Charlene instinctively liked her.

'Come in,' she said.

She realised that this was the woman whose husband they had met in the elevator. She'd been a model and a dancer, and although she was no longer young her movements were still graceful.

As they shared coffee, she looked Charlene up and down and said frankly, 'Thank heavens the rumours are true. They say he's found a nice girl who'll do him a lot of good and no harm. Good for you!'

'Thank you,' Charlene said.

'Of course you know the story about the dancer who descended on him at that party. She did it on purpose. I never liked her.'

'You know her?'

'I used to give lessons to girls who were going to dance in front of the camera. At least it was called dancing, but mostly it was sexy wriggling. She was one of my pupils.' She added hastily, 'But don't tell Travis.'

'I promise.' Charlene laughed. 'But about those lessons, you mean you can teach that sort of thing?'

'There are certain tricks, depending on how provocative you want to be.' She noticed a definite look in Charlene's eyes and asked teasingly, 'Want to try?'

She was about to decline when the daring imp who seemed to pop up in her mind a lot these days said, *Go on. Be a devil.*

'Yes,' she said. 'I'd like to give it a try.'

'Like this,' Rita said, and went into a wriggling dance that still contained much of her old ability.

She laughed as she danced, obviously enjoying the joke, and Charlene laughed too as she imitated her.

'Put your hands up high over your head so that people can see your body moving,' Rita advised.

'Like that?'

'Fine. Now imagine that the man you're dancing for is sitting in that chair over there. Approach him slinkily—good, that's right, but move your bottom more. You have to twist and squirm a bit—more, more—you're getting the hang of it. Now try to twirl and writhe at the same time. *Well done!*'

Laughing, Charlene spun around, moving so fast

that she lost track of the room whirling about her, and didn't see the door open, admitting Travis. Next moment she lost her balance and felt herself falling.

'Aaaah!' she cried.

'It's all right, I've got you.'

It was Travis's comforting voice, and Travis's steady arms enclosing her. But she'd collided with him so hard that he too lost his balance and fell into the chair with her in his lap.

'OK.' He laughed. 'The worst is over now.'

'Well,' Rita said, arms akimbo, 'that's one way of getting onto the guy's lap. Not one I've seen before, but I guess it works.'

'Hello, Rita,' Travis said. 'What are you two up to?'

'Rita was teaching me lap dancing,' Charlene said breathlessly.

'Really? Planning to take up a new career?'

'You never know,' she retorted. 'It's good to try anything once.'

'And she's got a real gift for it,' Rita added.

'Yeah, the gift of knocking a guy flying,' Travis said with a grin. 'I've come across it before.' He rubbed his back.

'I'm sorry,' Charlene said. 'Let me do that for you.'

She reached for him but he veered away. 'No need. I'll manage. You're a wicked woman. Rita, don't teach her any more dangerous tricks. She's beginning to scare me.'

'Nonsense, I've always scared you,' Charlene retorted, and the three of them shared a laugh.

'You know what you should do,' Rita said. 'Go back to that nightclub where *it* happened—'

'Not in a million years,' Travis said at once.

'No, wait. Take Charlene with you, and if those floozies start their nonsense again she'll show that she can do it even better than they can.'

'Hey, that's an idea,' Charlene said, fascinated.

'No,' Travis said quietly.

Rita beamed at Charlene. 'I'll need to teach you a bit more so that you're really expert—'

'I said no,' Travis snapped.

In the silence that followed they both looked at him, puzzled. That Travis, a man known for his sweet temper, should speak in that way was astonishing.

'I'm sorry,' he said, recovering himself quickly. 'It's been a long, hard day and I'm not at my best.'

'I'll be off now,' Rita said. 'I only came to return your book.'

She pushed it towards him, blew them both a kiss, and was gone.

'Did it go well today?' Charlene asked.

'Not too good. I've got a bad headache. I'll go straight to bed.'

'Let me get you something to eat.'

'No, thanks.' His words were tense and his smile forced. 'I just need to sleep. Goodnight.'

He vanished into his room, leaving Charlene staring at the closed door, frowning.

Why was Travis cross with her?

Ah, well, she thought at last. His headache must be worse than he'd said.

Travis lay awake for a long time. Something had happened that he needed to come to terms with, if he only knew how.

The moment when Charlene had landed in his lap was still with him. Her wriggling movements had been innocent, he knew. She'd been trying to steady herself, not inflame his senses, but she'd inflamed them nonetheless. The awareness of her body was burned into his flesh: searing, alarming, impossible to remove.

He'd never dreamed of this. Her plain looks had tricked him into thinking that the rest of her was the same. But now he knew otherwise, he thought, groaning as he remembered the enticing way she had moved against him, almost caressing him. Beneath her usually unrevealing clothes was a truly lovely body, one that he wanted to see as well as touch. The alarming discovery had been the reason he'd snapped at them, driven to distraction by the effort to keep himself under control while Rita joked about Charlene's sensual possibilities.

He groaned as he felt desire singing through his body, ignoring his attempts to silence it. He no longer knew the woman living in his home. She was a new, different Charlene, one he'd never imagined before.

One thing was clear. She must never know. His desire violated every promise he'd made to her. It also, he realised, broke her own promises about keeping everything sisterly. But in her innocence she had no idea about that. Nor would he allow her to suspect.

Over breakfast next morning his phone rang. As

soon as he answered, his face brightened. '*Mom!* You're coming home? Great. Tomorrow. We'll be at the airport. Yes, both of us. You can meet Charlene and I can meet—what did you say his name was? Sure I'm cheeky. I always was.'

He hung up, saying, 'You probably gathered what that was about. I told you my mom leads a colourful life.'

'With plenty of "gentleman friends"?'

'Definitely. She's been on vacation in Paris with Eric, the latest, and they're returning tomorrow.'

They were there early next day. To pass the time Travis bought a magazine and flicked through it casually until he came to something that made him stare.

Glancing over his shoulder, Charlene saw a young woman, scantily dressed, stretched out on a sofa. Her figure was curvaceous and magnificent, but that wasn't her chief attraction. It was more the look in her eyes as they gazed into the camera, a look that said, *Why don't we get together and...see what happens?*

She felt mildly insulted. If Travis expected her to play the role of the faithful girlfriend it was hardly courteous of him to slaver over another female in public.

'Hmm,' she said.

Glancing up, he read her thoughts. 'No, no, it's not what you think. That's Cassie.'

'Cassie? The one who—?'

'The girl Marcel wants to marry, and who told him to take a running jump. I did hear a rumour that she'd once had a career as a glamour model—'

'She seems to have returned to it.'

'And how! Poor Marcel.' Travis sighed. 'I shouldn't think he'll get her back now.'

'I wonder how much they paid her for that,' Charlene mused. 'Enough to buy her a lot of independence.'

'Is that all you see?' he demanded, comically outraged. 'Money?'

'It matters. When we're finished, I think I'll buy myself a toy boy.'

'He wouldn't be called Lee, would he?' Travis asked lightly. He knew he shouldn't have asked the question, but since the other night something mysterious seemed to have happened to his self-control.

'Lee? No way. He's in the past. But of course—'

she studied the picture again '—if I looked like her I wouldn't need to pay. The men would be clamouring to enjoy my charms.'

'It's not just voluptuous women who make men clamour,' he observed. 'There are other things that can be enchanting.'

'Nonsense!' she teased. 'That's just polite male talk. What all of you actually think is that real women are plump and luscious. The rest of us are too skinny to count.'

'Oh, that's what men think, is it?' he asked, raising his eyebrows.

'Sure is.'

'And who made you an expert in male thinking?'

'Women are born knowing it. And if they don't, they soon find out.'

He cocked his head on one side. 'So you're going to lecture me on the subject?'

'Why not? Since we're brother and sister, I can say what I like to you.'

'Brother and sister,' he murmured.

'It's what we agreed. That way, we're both safe.'

'Then, since we're speaking frankly, let me tell you that you don't know half what you think you do. Some men like to be taken by surprise.'

That made her gaze at him, wondering about his meaning and the slight edge in his voice. But then the loudspeaker shrieked, *'The flight from Paris has landed—'*

The moment collapsed and died. It was time to get back to real life.

Whatever that was.

Julia Franklin still looked much as Charlene remembered her from old films on television. Though well into her fifties, she could have passed for forty or less, the result, Charlene guessed, of much cosmetic surgery and sessions in the gym. It was the same with her charm, which was untouched by the years.

She greeted Travis with an eager cry of, *'Darling!'* shrieked over a distance, and began to run. He did the same and they threw themselves into each other's arms, to the delight of the crowd, most of whom had recognised Travis.

Behind Julia came a man in his thirties, with a cherubic face and a good-natured air. This must be Eric, Charlene thought. Travis greeted him amiably, but with the caution of a man who'd met too many of his predecessors.

A cab took them to Bunker Hill, where Julia

lived in a house that was defiantly colourful and un-modern. From the first moment Charlene felt herself under inspection. Julia had clearly heard the talk and was buzzing with curiosity.

'I haven't told her everything about us,' Travis had said earlier. 'Only that we met by accident in the studio, and found we could talk to each other easily. She doesn't know anything about Lee.'

During the meal, Julia dominated the conversation, talking about Paris and Rome, where she and Eric had spent their vacation. Eric sat looking at Julia with a little smile on his face.

Afterwards, Julia drew Charlene aside, saying, 'Come and have lunch here tomorrow. We'll do much better without the men.' Her voice became teasing. 'I think we always do better without men, don't you?'

'Sometimes.' Charlene laughed. 'But they come in handy now and then.'

'Good thinking,' Julia said triumphantly.

Later, Julia pulled her son into the kitchen and shut the door.

'So that's her. That's really her. I've been dying to meet her, although I've seen so many pictures of the two of you that I almost feel I know her. Look at that.'

She held up the snap taken in the hotel restaurant, showing Charlene convulsed with laughter.

'I'd bought her some pearl earrings,' Travis recalled, 'but I'd also bought some Daft Doody earrings for a friend, and I got muddled and gave her the wrong ones.'

'And she saw the funny side of that?' Julia asked, amazed.

'As you see.'

'Then she's a real jewel.' She eyed him with motherly suspicion. 'You do realise that, don't you?'

'Oh, yes,' he murmured. 'I realise that. Mom, can we talk about this later? I have a lot to tell you.'

'And I've got a lot to tell you. Paris was fantastic, and guess what! I bumped into your father. I was invited to some big reception, and there he was. Marcel was there too. Poor soul, he's so sad since he broke up with Cassie. He sent you his good wishes.'

'I'll bet my father didn't send me any good wishes.'

'Actually, he was on his best behaviour because Freya was there.'

'Freya? She's his stepdaughter by his new wife, isn't she?'

'Yes, and she's really very nice. Amos has set his heart on marrying her to one of his sons. He failed with Darius, so now he wants it to be Marcel. You should be careful. If he fails with Marcel he'll get you in his sights.'

'Hey, c'mon!'

'Really. "The Falcon" never gives up. That's what they say.'

'Then I'll have to set Charlene onto him. If that doesn't fill him with fear, nothing will.'

Which left Julia regarding him oddly and mulling over the conversation long into the night, so that Eric was roused to ask if anything was wrong.

'Nothing wrong,' she murmured. 'Just something I can't make up my mind about.'

'Would a cuddle help?'

'Yes, please!'

CHAPTER EIGHT

NEXT day Charlene paid Julia a visit. The two women liked each other. Julia was no actress. The cheeky kid she'd played as a starlet was simply her real self, and after thirty years she still existed. For much of the meal they swapped witticisms, but they both wanted to talk about Travis, and at last Julia said, 'He was always a lovely boy. So sweet-natured and full of feeling. I used to wish he didn't have so many feelings, so that his father couldn't hurt him so much.'

'He really minded about that, didn't he? He didn't say much but I could sense rivers running deep underneath.'

Julia nodded, then went to a cupboard and brought out a large book, which she opened, revealing a portrait photograph of Amos Falcon.

'I took this shot of him when we knew each other, years ago,' she said.

Amos had been an attractive man, not conventionally handsome, but with a fierce purpose in his face that proclaimed him one of life's winners. Many women would find that appealing, as the young Julia had done.

As she still did, Charlene thought, watching the other woman as she surveyed the photograph. After all this time, there was sadness and longing in her face as she flipped over the pages to find pictures of the two of them together. Amos and Julia, a young girl, her face full of love, happy in the conviction that she had found her man and they would be together for ever.

More pictures: Julia with baby Travis in her arms, but never the three of them together.

'Are there any of Amos and Travis together?' she asked.

'None,' Julia said. 'That's one thing I can't forgive Amos for. He paid maintenance for Travis, but he never took any real interest in him. He'd visit, talk to him about how he was doing at school, criticise him. But he wouldn't pose for a picture or become really involved with him. But look at these.'

At the back of the book were newspaper cuttings showing Amos with some of his other sons.

'Darius, Jackson, Marcel,' Julia said bitterly. 'But

not Travis. I've seen him looking at these pictures with such sadness. Just imagine what he must have been thinking.'

'That they were a complete family without him,' Charlene whispered. 'How well I know that feeling.'

'Then you understand how it's been for him. I'm so glad.'

'It was much the same for me,' Charlene said.

Briefly she outlined the situation in her own family.

'I'm lucky in my grandparents. I get on with them wonderfully, and thank goodness I do because they're all I've got.'

'And I'm all Travis has got,' Julia said. 'I have no relatives. I'm an orphan, raised in an institution.' She gave a grim laugh. 'You wouldn't believe it, would you? The big star, the world at his feet, women pursuing him, but it breaks his heart that he's never felt really included in a family.

'I haven't been as good a mother as I meant to be,' she added wryly. 'At one time I thought I'd marry and give him a father, but none of my relationships ever quite worked out and…well, it didn't increase stability, if you see what I mean.'

Charlene nodded, liking Julia even more for the honesty with which she admitted her own failings.

'But he's got you,' Julia went on. 'He hasn't said much, but I gather you're protecting him from the people who are out to harm him. I can see that he's close to you, much closer than to women he sleeps with. Sometimes sex can actually form a barrier to closeness.'

She took Charlene's hand. 'Just be there for him,' she said. 'I know you will be, and I thank you with all my heart.'

'I'll be there,' Charlene promised.

Soon after that Travis arrived to collect her, looking from one to the other, smiling when he sensed the warmth and friendliness.

As soon as she could, Julia drew him aside, murmuring, 'Now I can have an easy mind about you. And I never thought I'd say that.'

'Mom, it's not like that. She's a friend.'

'A friend who happens to be living with you. A friend the whole world is talking about.'

'That's just it. We want the world to be talking about her so that they forget what happened in the nightclub. I couldn't face losing all I'd gained. Luckily Charlene agreed to help me.'

'How much does she know?'

'Everything. I didn't lie to her. That's the most wonderful thing about her. You can be completely honest and trust her to understand. It's such a relief.'

'Someone you can be completely open with. That's more luck than most people ever have. And you actually persuaded her to put on a big performance for the cameras?'

'Yes.'

'And the fact that you're living together isn't—?'

'No.'

'And you're not—?'

'No!'

'And you haven't even tried to—?'

'No!'

She surveyed him, half cynical, half amused.

'I don't think you're my son at all. You're an impostor. What have you done with the real Travis?'

He grinned. 'He decided to lie low for a while. He reckons he isn't so clever.'

She patted his hand. 'Well, getting Charlene to help you was really clever. She'll do you the world of good. You might start appreciating other things about women than the shape of their behinds. Why, darling, you're blushing!'

'Nonsense!' he said hurriedly. 'Can we leave it?'

'Of course. I'll just say this. I think she's the woman for you, and you should try to win her for life.'

'Mom, please. You just don't understand.'

She patted his face. 'No, my darling. It's you that doesn't understand.'

Life settled into a comfortable pattern. Sometimes they would go out together, always choosing a place where they would be seen and enjoying the public reaction, whether it appeared in the press or on the Internet.

'But don't overdo it,' Joe, the Press Officer, had warned. 'The public are quite sophisticated about this kind of thing these days, and if you live in each other's pockets they suspect a PR stunt.'

With one voice they exclaimed, *'Shocking!'*

Joe grinned. 'You two scare me sometimes. It's like the same brain working both of you!'

They shared a smile. Their instinctive mental harmony was a source of pleasure to them.

But they heeded Joe's words, and went out separately. She enjoyed the theatre, while he preferred to spend an evening with friends. She wondered if the friends included the kind of ladies he didn't dare be seen with, but if so he never mentioned it. When describing his evening he would finish with, 'I was boringly virtuous. You'd have been proud of me.'

'You could tell me if anything happened,' she said once. 'I wouldn't be jealous.'

'And I would tell you, if there was anything to tell. You'd need to be warned, for practical reasons.'

And since she had a deep belief in the trust between them, she accepted his word.

One evening Travis arrived home to find her about to leave.

'Going somewhere interesting?'

'To the theatre, with some of the girls from the TV studio. There's six of us going in total. It's an open air performance, so I'm just dressed casual.'

He noticed that by 'just casual' she meant the tight jeans she'd been wearing the day she sat on his lap, when he—

He shut off the thought.

From below came a beep from a horn.

'That's my taxi,' she said. 'Right, I'll be off.'

'Will you be late?'

'Very late, probably.' She added significantly, 'And I promise to come in quietly.'

He understood. She was saying that he was free to enjoy himself with another woman—or women.

'Charlene—'

'Got to dash. Bye!'

She blew him a kiss, and was gone.

From the window he watched her hop merrily into the taxi. As he turned back into the room he realised how empty it was. How silent and lonely.

Suddenly it was intolerable. He ran swiftly through a list of female names, seeking one that would do. The problem was that there were so many that would 'do'. Too many.

His choice fell on Susie. They were old friends and she liked nothing better than to have a good time, with nothing serious on either side, except a generous gift to finish the evening. He picked up the phone.

As soon as she heard his voice she cried, '*Darling!* It's been a long time.'

'How about we put that right? Are you free this evening?'

'I am for you. Where shall we meet?'

'Why don't you come over here?'

She gave a knowing laugh. 'That sounds lovely. Who needs other people?'

They understood each other perfectly.

Charlene's evening out was short-lived. The play was poor, the acting terrible. In the interval she and her friends poured out and headed into the nearest restaurant.

'Hey, look who's there!' exclaimed a young woman. 'Penny Danes. She's the TV star in *The Man From Heaven.* Who's that handsome guy snuggling up to her?'

'His name's Lee Anton,' Charlene said. 'He's just started in the series.'

Cameras were flashing on the theatrically loving couple. Penny stretched out her hand, flaunting a ring, then kissed Lee, waving the ring again.

'Looks like they've got engaged,' someone observed. 'Do you know him, Charlene?'

'No,' she said quietly. 'I don't know him.'

Soon after that she discovered that she was tired. Bidding goodnight to her companions, she slipped quietly away and went to stand outside the restaurant, looking in at Lee and his new lover.

It should have hurt, she thought wryly, but that was all over. Now she had a new life, thanks to Travis, with his gift of touching her emotions. Their relationship might only be friendly, but so few people had ever bothered with her emotions in the past that it could be dangerous if she wasn't careful.

But I am careful, she thought. *Careful is my middle name. He's my dear brother, and I won't let anything spoil it.*

She turned and went to hail a taxi. Nothing appeared and after a while she thought of going back inside. But when she turned, Lee was standing there.

'Fancy seeing you! Come in and meet my fiancée.'

'Thank you, no. But I wish you every happiness, Lee.'

'You don't blame me, then?'

'Why should I blame you? There was nothing really between us.'

She had the feeling that this didn't please him.

'Anyway, I hope Travis doesn't hurt you too

much when your break-up comes. And it will. He's not known as a faithful guy. The girls love him, but he doesn't love them. Since he linked up with you they say he's a reformed character.' He eyed her hilariously. 'But I guess you'd know about that.'

'I see a taxi,' she said hurriedly. 'Goodnight, Lee.'

She couldn't get away from him fast enough.

It was dark when she reached home. She let herself in quietly, meaning to tiptoe to her room, unnoticed. But the door to Travis's bedroom was ajar, and from behind it she could hear a woman's voice.

'Oh, darling, you're so sweet. If only other people saw the real you—knew you as I do—'

Silence. Charlene was tense, waiting for his voice, wondering what he would say.

'It's better if they don't,' he said at last. 'Let's keep it our secret.'

'Oh, yes, of course you're right. This is special to us—'

Charlene flattened herself against the wall, her eyes darting frantically from side to side. There was no way to reach her own room without passing the open door, and the thought of being discovered like this made her quail.

But the alternative was to stay concealed, effectively spying on Travis.

Help! wailed a voice in her head. *I can't handle this.*

'I've really missed you,' came the female voice again. 'And you've missed me. I can tell. You have, haven't you?'

Heart pounding, Charlene waited for his answer, but instead of words there came only a *Mmm* sound, suggesting a prolonged kiss.

'Travis—'

'Wait.' That was his voice.

He was moving about the room. Charlene held her breath as she sensed him grow nearer. Even so, she wasn't prepared for the moment when he came into sight. The door was open just wide enough to show the whole of him, naked except for a pair of black briefs, so tiny they were almost non-existent.

She drew back into the shadows as far as she could go, unable to take her eyes off him. That a man so tall and lean should yet have such perfectly formed muscles, such a hint of restrained power, such beauty. She could hardly believe what her eyes were telling her.

He seemed preoccupied with troublesome

thoughts, which was strange if he was on the verge of making love to his companion. He turned, showing his body from a new angle, the gentle swell of his rear, the length of his thighs.

At last he moved away behind the door, and she seized the chance to creep to her room. She didn't even put the light on. At all costs he mustn't suspect that she'd returned. She could feel her heart beating so fiercely that she feared he must be able to hear even at that distance.

She undressed quickly and got into bed, diving beneath the cover as though seeking shelter. The whole world seemed to have rocked. It was disgraceful to have seen his near nakedness while he was unaware, but she couldn't make herself regret it. Even now he walked through her thoughts, casually magnificent.

But he wasn't alone. A young woman was with him, lying in his bed, waiting for him to approach her. Obviously he'd called her as soon as she herself had gone out for the evening.

Lee's words came back to her. *The girls love him, but he doesn't love them.*

She had no right to complain. She'd promised to come in quietly in case he had a girl. But somehow she hadn't really believed it, and the reality came as a shock.

She rolled over, burying her face in the pillow.

'Don't you care for me any more?' Susie's soft voice was petulant.

'What do you mean?'

'Usually by this time you've tossed me on the bed and—' She finished with a significant little giggle.

'A man learns patience as he gets older,' he said with a touch of desperation.

'But don't I attract you?'

'Of course you do,' he said determinedly. 'You're as lovely as ever. It's just that—'

He fought for something to say. Anything would do, other than the truth, which was that inviting her here tonight had been the biggest mistake he'd ever made, and he was paying for it. He'd watched as she undressed, waiting for the moment when his excitement rose, but nothing had happened.

Nor had it happened when she removed his own clothes. Her touch, her voluptuous charms left him unmoved.

Disaster!

If only he could banish the cheeky ghost that lingered in the apartment, a ghost who teased him as a sister, who'd shown him a whole new side of life, even made him see himself in a new light. A ghost with a tempting body that she kept concealed from the world so that only the privileged were allowed to discover it.

And who was out tonight—doing what? And with whom?

'What is it?' Susie demanded. 'You suddenly jumped as though you'd seen a ghost.'

'I think I did,' he said, seizing inspiration quickly. 'It's Charlene—she could come back at any moment—'

'But you said she'd be gone a long time.'

'I could be wrong. I'm sorry, I'm not at my best. I think we should forget this.'

'Well, really! What a way to treat a lady!'

He'd never seen Susie in a temper before, and it wasn't a pretty sight. After spitting out a few curses, she declared significantly, 'I don't like wasting my time.'

'Of course you don't,' he placated her, 'but I have a present for you. Here.'

He took a bracelet from a drawer where he'd left

it, awaiting the right moment to give it to Charlene. Mollified, Susie let him put it on her wrist.

'That's more like it,' she said. 'And next time maybe we'll have more luck.'

There wasn't going to be a next time but he was too wise to say so.

'Goodbye, Susie.'

She stalked out of the bedroom towards the front door, which he held open for her. There she turned to give him a beguiling smile, to remind him what he was missing. But, to her annoyance, he wasn't looking at her. His attention had been caught by something a few feet away, and it seemed to astound him.

'Goodbye,' she snapped.

He didn't reply, merely closing the door without taking his eyes from whatever had caught them. Susie flounced on her way.

Travis was too dazed to move. What he'd seen had stunned him with its implications. There, on a small table, was Charlene's purse.

She'd taken it with her. It shouldn't be here.

But it was.

Which meant that she was here too. She must have come in while he was with Susie, and slipped quietly into her room, passing his bedroom door, which had been standing open.

And she'd seen—?

What?

After struggling with himself for what felt like ages, he tapped on her door.

'Hello?' came her voice.

'It's me.'

The door opened, revealing her in an all covering robe.

'You left your purse out here,' he said, holding it up.

'Oh, I…didn't notice…' She seemed as distracted as himself. 'Thank you.'

He waited for her to stand back and invite him in. But she didn't.

'I wasn't expecting you back as soon as this,' he said lamely.

'The play was a disaster. I came home early.'

So she was pretending not to know about Susie, he thought. But he wasn't fooled. There was no way she couldn't know.

'I had a friend over,' he said casually.

'Good. I hope it was fun. I expect you're worn out now.'

Clearly she thought he'd been making love to Susie, and equally clearly it didn't bother her.

That was good, he admonished himself. *Brother and sister. Don't forget.*

'No, I'm not worn out,' he said. 'It wasn't *that* much of a fun evening.'

After a brief pause, she asked, 'Really?'

'Really,' he said firmly.

She managed a faint smile. 'I'm disappointed in you.'

'So was the lady. I don't think I met her expectations. Suddenly I wasn't interested, and there are some things that…well, you just can't pretend.'

It hurt her to see the strain in his face.

'It'll be better next time,' she murmured. 'There are so many other girls.'

'When you're young and stupid perhaps. But in the end it has to be the right one.'

'But you are young. You aren't thirty yet.'

'Suddenly I don't feel young any more. Hey, guess what! Maybe I grew up. I wonder what made that happen.'

Travis was on the edge of a precipice, saying things he should never have dared say to her, but he didn't know how to stop.

'Don't listen to me; I'm talking nonsense,' he hurried to say.

'That's all right. You can say anything to your big sister.'

As often before, she reached out to lay a gentle hand against his cheek. Travis laid his own hand over it but didn't look up to meet her eyes. His gaze seemed fixed on his feet.

'It's late,' he said at last. 'Time we were getting some sleep. I'm sorry I disturbed you.'

'Yes, of course,' she said, disappointed. 'Good-night.'

She closed the door. Whatever he'd been about to say would not now be said. What he might have done would be left undone. She sighed.

Travis stood in the dark hall for a moment, then backed away, knowing he must get as far from her as possible and silence the raging tremors that went through his body. What Susie's flaunting sexuality had failed to do, Charlene's lightest touch on his cheek had done with ease. For the second time that night his mind said *Disaster*, but for a different reason.

When he remembered how he'd admitted his own failure to her he wanted to vanish into thin air. Instead, he curled up in bed, pulled the covers over his head and tried to pretend he didn't exist.

In her own room, Charlene got slowly into bed, disturbed by a thousand conflicting instincts. But she couldn't cope with them. She must try to escape into sleep. She closed her eyes and headed for the safety of oblivion.

Looking back at what happened next, she supposed she should have seen it coming. It was as inevitable as the rising of the sun, but she didn't understand that at the time.

Her dreams were vague, just impressions floating through her mind, until suddenly Travis appeared.

Time had turned back and they were talking together in warmth and friendship. He touched her cheek, a sign of warmth that they frequently exchanged. It was the lightest gesture and she had responded to it happily—laughing, pleased but unruffled.

But now that touch was happening again in her dreams, and her flesh was reacting as it hadn't done before. Suddenly she was responding with all her heart, relishing their emotional closeness and understanding, but above all rejoicing in his touch.

It was there again, his hand moving softly against her skin, tempting her to reach up, clasp it, drawing it further down. His eyes were telling her that this was what he wanted, if only she—

Charlene awoke with a cry, finding herself sitting up in bed, staring into the darkness, appalled at herself. Everything she remembered, the urgency in his caress, the vibrancy of her response—*these things hadn't happened!*

Except perhaps deep inside, hidden out of sight in some remote place where neither her mind nor her feelings were in control.

Mysteriously, her body had stored up the memory, waiting until she was ready to confront it, then releasing it now, when her heart was suddenly open to him and she had no defences to protect her from its dangerous message.

No, she told herself, trying to be firm. *I'm imagining things. Just a pathetic fantasist telling herself what she wants to believe.*

Travis's voice came from behind the door. 'Charlene—Charlie—? What's happened?'

'Nothing, I'm fine,' she forced herself to call back.

'Are you sure? I thought I heard you cry out.'

'I was out of bed,' she stammered. 'I stubbed my toe.'

'Can I come in?'

'No,' she cried quickly. 'Goodnight.'

'Goodnight.' He sounded reluctant, but at last she heard him move away.

She lay there, breathing hard, trying to pull herself together, but with no success. Where was calm, sensible Charlie when she was needed? Nowhere to be found.

But she was strong. She wouldn't give in to her sudden fierce awareness of him as a man. That was her problem, not his, and he mustn't be allowed to suspect. She closed her eyes, trying to banish him.

Yet he was stubborn and awkward, lingering on the edge of her consciousness, demanding entry to remind her once more how her heart was eagerly opening to him, reproaching her for not feeling it before.

'No,' she cried desperately. 'You mustn't— *I* mustn't— No, *please*!"

'Charlie!'

'No—no—'

'Charlie—wake up!'

She could feel his hands, grasping her firmly

until she opened her eyes and realised that Travis had come into the room. He was sitting on the bed, holding her shoulders and giving her a gentle shake.

'Wake up,' he said. 'Charlie, please wake up.'

'Oh—yes—yes—'

'Are you awake now?'

'Yes,' she choked.

'My poor dear. Such a terrible nightmare you must have had. You sounded in agony.'

'You could hear me?' she cried, aghast. Whatever had she said? What had she revealed?

'I could hear you in my room, through two closed doors. I know you sent me away before but I couldn't leave you to suffer alone like that. I heard you call, "I mustn't—no, please". What's so terrible that you mustn't do it? Come on, you can tell me. I'm your brother, remember?'

That was the one thing he would never be again, she thought desperately. He was a man, with all a man's attractions. She'd deluded herself about this before, but never again.

Now he was lying down on the bed, his arms about her in a hug that devastated her with its hint of things she might yearn for but could never claim.

The blankets were between them and she clung to that thought for safety, because she so desperately wished that they weren't. Even so, she could feel the shape of his body, its warmth and power, its promise of delight for a woman he had chosen.

But she was not that woman. He hadn't chosen her. He'd turned to her in despair.

'What was the dream about?' he whispered.

'I'm…not sure. It was so vague—'

'But you sounded scared. You were pleading. Who were you pleading with?'

I was pleading with myself not to fall in love with you, pleading for strength and common sense to save me from what I want so much.

'Nobody,' she said. 'Nothing.'

'You're lying. Why? What is it that you can't tell me?'

I can never tell you anything again.

'I can't remember,' she forced herself to say. 'It's over now. I can go back to sleep.'

'You want me to go?'

'You've got a long day tomorrow,' she said with an attempt at brightness. 'You must think of that.'

'I see. All right, I'll go.'

There was a faintly forlorn note in his voice,

almost as though he felt snubbed. But she barely heard it through her own feeling of rejection. She waited until he'd gone, then rolled over and curled up in a ball, as though trying to shut out the whole world. She stayed like that, wide awake and fretting, for the rest of the night.

CHAPTER NINE

NEXT morning she told him about Lee and Penny's engagement.

'Oh, Charlie, I'm sorry. Was it very painful for you?'

'Not at all. Over and done with.'

'The one I'm sorry for is Penny,' he mused. 'Her contract has just been renewed for next season's show. So far, his hasn't. But with her to fight his corner—' He shrugged.

'Let's hope things work out well for them both,' she said.

It was strange to recall how this would once have broken her heart, but that was before her new awareness of Travis as a man. While it was only his kind friendship that had touched her it had been easy to keep a sense of proportion. But since she'd seen him nearly naked everything had been different.

'What is it?' he asked suddenly.

'What's what?'

'That look on your face, as though you'd discovered a secret joke. What have I said that's funny?'

'Nothing. It's not you that's funny. It's me.'

'So tell me.'

'No…no, I can't,' she insisted.

'All right, I don't want to pry. By the way, I'm sorry about last night.'

'But what is there to be sorry about?'

'Getting all miserable and emotional. I went too far. You do know you've got nothing to fear from me, don't you?'

'Yes,' she said with a touch of sadness. 'I do know.'

'I promised you that when you moved in here—' he gave a self-conscious laugh '—when I more or less forced you to move in.'

'You didn't force me.'

'Manipulated you, then. I seized the chance to make you do what suited me. I'm good at that, I'm afraid, and I don't blame you if you don't trust me. I wouldn't trust me. I'm a bad character. But you know that.'

'Travis, there's no need for this, honestly.'

'All right, I'll shut up in a minute. I talk too much as well.'

That was true. If she hadn't been distracted by her own nerves she might have noticed that he was gabbling like a man holding on for dear life.

'You're probably planning to make a run for it,' he went on, 'but there's no need. I give you my word. Don't leave me, Charlie.'

'I won't leave. I know you can't manage without your big sister.'

'Funny how you always say *big* sister, although I'm older than you.'

'No, you're not. Compared to me, you're about five years old.'

He gave a rueful grin. 'I guess that's true. What would I do without you to keep me on the straight and narrow?'

'You'd pick someone else from the crowds who'd apply.'

'But there aren't crowds because nobody else knows that much about me. I'd never let them. Only you.'

'Well, be careful how many of your dark secrets you tell me. When this is over I'll probably blackmail you.'

They both laughed, but then he said, 'Why should it be over? Why can't we stay in touch for the rest of our lives? You're the best friend I ever had, and I'm not going to let my best friend go.'

Best friend. Once the words would have pleased her. Now they were like the crack of doom.

The phone rang. He answered it and a moment later she heard him cry, *'Yes!'* in a voice full of delight. 'That's wonderful! I don't know what took you so long—yes, yes, all right. Of course I'm coming. I wouldn't miss it for the world. Give Cassie my love.'

He hung up, seized Charlene and waltzed her around the room.

'What's happened?' she asked, laughing.

'That was my brother, Marcel.'

'The one who made a mess of his proposal and she went back to modelling?'

'That's the one. But he's got her back. You remember that picture we saw, and you said she must be making a lot of money? Well, she was, enough to invest in his business. Then she marched in, told him she was a fellow shareholder.'

'So he had to treat her as an equal instead of walking all over her,' Charlene said. 'Excellent.'

'Somehow they've managed to get it together, and they're marrying in Paris next month. It'll be a big celebration. We'll have a great time, and you can meet my family.'

'Am I invited?'

'Are you—? Listen, everyone's crazy to meet you. I wouldn't dare go without you. Hang it! Who's that?' The phone had rung again. 'Yes? Hi, Joe. Yes, I'm on my way—glad you're pleased—well, I guess we could do some more—wait, she's here. I'll ask her.'

He turned to Charlene. 'It's Joe. He's pleased with the story so far, but he wants to "direct strategy" as he puts it. Can you come into the studio with me this morning?'

'Sure.'

'Joe, we're on our way.'

Joe cornered them as soon as they arrived and swept them down to the studio canteen. By now Charlene was used to being surveyed, and wasn't offended by the way he looked her up and down, then nodded.

'Yup. Going well.'

'Thank you,' she said ironically.

'No, really, you're doing a fantastic job.'

'What about me?' Travis demanded comically.

'Oh, sure, you too.'

Travis put his arm around Charlene's shoulder, hugging her and saying, 'You see how it is. Now you're here nobody notices me any more. I could get insulted.'

'Yeah, right.' She aimed a shadow punch at him. He delighted her in this jokey mood.

'Can we be serious?' Joe demanded. 'I know the press are in pursuit but we need to stage something where we're in control. I've arranged a theatre attendance for you so that they can see you entering the box, standing there for all to see. And I think a couple of shopping expeditions. Travis, you should buy her some jewellery so that'll start them speculating.'

'Do we want them to speculate?' Charlene asked. 'What happens when it comes to nothing?'

'Who says it comes to nothing?' Joe asked.

'That's enough,' Travis said firmly. 'Don't go too far. Charlene's helping us out of the goodness of her heart.'

'And she'll gain. You can give her a lot of jewellery, all paid for by the studio, and if you eventually quarrel and she chucks it back at you, I'll make sure it's returned to her quietly.'

'Oh, we quarrel and I chuck it back at him?' she said hilariously.

'Yeah, but be careful how you do that. Don't hit his face. The studio has a lot of money invested in that face.'

'Fine, I'll just punch him in the stomach.'

'You're enjoying this, aren't you?' Travis asked wildly.

'I don't know how I'm keeping a straight face,' she told him.

'Yeah, it's got its funny side,' Joe conceded with a grin, 'but it's serious too. I shouldn't be telling you this quite so soon but—' he lowered his voice '—it's just possible that the series will be turned into a film.'

They both stared at him, dumbstruck.

'A film?' Travis whispered.

'Right. And you're the leading candidate for the part.'

'He should be the only candidate,' Charlene said indignantly. 'He made it what it is.'

'And that's why we're backing him all the way,' Joe said. 'But Alaric Lanley is interested.'

The other two drew sharp breaths. Lanley was a major film star.

'If he wants it they'll give it to him,' Travis said.

'Not necessarily. Like Charlene says, it's you that's associated with the part, and that's worth money. Have you ever met Alaric, by the way?'

'Yes, once at a party,' Travis said. 'I thought he seemed a nice guy.'

'Well, don't let anyone hear you say that,' Joe said, scandalised. 'You're enemies. This is a fight to the death. Give a few interviews saying he'll steal your role at his peril. Nothing specific. Just some vague showbizzy threats.'

'Forget it,' Travis said at once.

'Look—'

'I said forget it. Excuse me.' He leaned sideways to attract the attention of a waitress.

While he was talking to her, Joe growled to Charlene, 'What can you do with this guy? There are things he just doesn't understand.'

'Yes,' she agreed, 'being nasty is something he definitely doesn't understand. Kicking people in the teeth, treating them badly because they've treated him badly. Don't try to change it. It makes him what he is.'

He gave her a look of appreciation. 'Guess you're right. Fine,' he resumed as Travis turned back to them, 'we've got to do some urgent PR work to keep you in front of the public at all times.

'It helps that we've got this big story about the two of you. So far it's been great. People have seen you in the street, in restaurants. But now we need to direct the public to what we want them to see.'

Charlene knew a moment's doubt. This almost military planning wasn't what she had agreed to. But then she saw Travis watching her uneasily, and knew that she had no choice. This was his big chance, and she'd promised to be here for him.

'Are you up for it?' Joe asked.

'Yes,' she said firmly.

'Yes,' Travis said, giving her a look of gratitude.

'Great. Then let's make plans.'

'What about a beach party?' Travis said. 'We gather on Venice Beach, swim, romp, dance around.'

'Great!' Joe exclaimed. 'I'll set it up and let you know.'

So that was that, Travis thought, mentally reclining with a sense of satisfaction. What he knew of Charlene's body came from sensations. He desperately needed to see the whole of her and marry the feelings up with visions. He'd been racking his brain for a way, and now one had been presented to him. A beach. Charlene in a bathing costume, everything laid out for his delighted inspection.

He knew a faint twinge of guilt. To trick her into displaying her body wasn't the act of a gentleman.

'Are you all right with this?' he asked her anxiously. 'I know you said yes to help me, but I wouldn't want to force you into anything.'

A picture swam into Charlene's vision: Travis as she'd seen him last night, naked but for the tiny trunks, just as he would be again on the beach.

'I think I can just about endure it,' she said.

Joe pursued his plans determinedly, announcing that their theatre seats had been booked for the following night.

'What's the show?' Travis asked.

'Um…hang on, I'll check.'

He scanned a newspaper, prompting Travis to ask in an appalled tone, 'You booked the play without knowing what it was?'

'It's a great theatre with a huge box where everyone will see you. What does the play matter? Here we are. *Seek the Nightmare*.'

They both jumped at the sound of the play that was notorious for being learned and mysterious.

'It was a big success in the West End of London,' Joe said. 'Charlene saw it there and loved it.'

'I did not,' she said indignantly. 'Not my sort of thing at all.'

'You loved it,' Joe said firmly. 'And Travis is taking you to it here as a special treat.'

'I'm glad you told me,' Travis said in a faint voice. 'I don't have to pretend to like it, do I?'

'You'll have to decide whether you're the gallant chevalier enduring it for the sake of his lady, or the dark-browed intellectual sunk in thought,' Joe told him.

Travis gave him a look. Charlene covered her quivering lips.

'And during the interval,' Joe continued, gathering his things, 'remember to talk. The press love that because they can imagine what you're saying, and write the script for themselves. "Has he asked her yet?" That kind of thing. All right, I'm off.'

He left them before either could speculate about what 'asking her' might mean.

On the night they wore evening clothes. Around her neck Charlene sported a diamond necklace, bought by the studio and glamorous enough to inspire questions. She didn't care. The actress in her was enjoying the game. And on her wrist she wore a bracelet, given to her by Travis with the words, 'I bought you a gift a few days ago but things have been so hectic I didn't give it until now.'

He reckoned that explanation would have to do, since he could hardly tell the truth, that it was a replacement for the one he'd had to give Susie to cover his embarrassment.

At the theatre they were applauded in the foyer and again when they made their entrance into the box. The play was officially 'intellectual', a dark, soul-searching work that made Charlene want to laugh derisively at its self-indulgence. But Joe was delighted with the reports he'd received from his spy in the stalls.

'You looked great and you talked to each other, so people could see you interacting,' he whooped.

'It's as well they couldn't hear the conversation.' She chuckled when they were alone.

'Yes, me threatening to leave if it got any more boring, and you promising to wake me up when it was over. That would have given Joe a heart attack.'

'Never mind. He won't find out. We're a team.'

'Yes,' he murmured, holding her hand. 'We are.'

The arrangements for the party on Venice Beach had been made with detailed precision.

'It's a day out for everyone,' Joe had explained. 'The whole cast, crew, director, we all decided to treat ourselves to a rest day, and the press just happened to find out. They'll be watching you two, walking, swimming, eating—whatever.'

'Are you sure you're all right with this?' Travis asked her again as they got ready to leave in the morning. 'You had an odd look on your face when Joe was describing it.'

'I was only worried in case I couldn't measure up.'

'You'll measure up. You're going to be wonderful, because you always are.'

Charlene spoke seriously. 'I hope I'm everything you want me to be, because I know how much this matters to you. I saw the look on your face too, only it wasn't a funny look. This was a man full of excitement because he could see the big chance coming up. But he was also just a little afraid in case he couldn't make the most of it.'

'How well you understand me.' Travis sighed. 'All the shields and defences that fool other people—you just see right through them as though they weren't there.' He took both her hands in his and kissed each one lightly. 'With anyone else that would scare me, but with you I know it's all right.' He added wryly, 'You only got one thing wrong.'

'What was that?'

'I'm not "just a little afraid". I'm scared stiff. To lose this chance—' he gave a brief laugh '—if I get that film part, it could lead to so much.'

'Yes, it would. There'd be a second film, and then a third, and studios would be falling over themselves to hire you.'

'I'd be so much bigger than I am now, and then perhaps—'

'Then even your father would have to give you some respect,' she said. 'Yes, he'll be proud of you, and boast about you. "Hey, my son is Travis Falcon."'

'Yup! That's it. It's stupid, isn't it? I'm a grown man, well, at least I pretend to be. I fool the others, but not you.'

'Maybe I have my own ideas of what constitutes a grown man,' she said.

'Lucky for me.'

'If he's kind and gentle, generous and caring, that's all I care about. You can stuff the macho business.'

'You don't think I'm making too much of today, do you?' he asked. 'It's only a few hours spent fooling for the camera—'

'It's not going to win the victory on its own,' she agreed. 'But it's a step on the road. Then you'll take another step, and another, until you're running so fast that nobody can catch you.'

'*We'll* be running,' he corrected.

'No, this is about you. I'm just backup. You'll be a big, *big* star and you'll make so much money that your father and your brothers will want to borrow from you.'

He grinned. 'In my dreams. But yes, that's where the road leads. I'll become obsessed with money, and then they'll know that I'm a real Falcon after all.' He added quietly, 'But do I want to travel that road?'

'You won't become obsessed with money,' she

told him. 'Not you. What you make of it is up to you. It'll be *your* road. *Your* decisions.'

'What about yours?'

'Yours,' she said firmly. 'Nobody else's.'

He looked at her for a moment, then drew her close, wrapping his arms right around her and holding her against him.

'What would I do without you?' he murmured against her hair. 'Don't leave me, because I couldn't bear that. I… You see, if I could only… Just don't leave me.'

She stroked his hair, deeply touched by what she'd seen inside him. Travis might say what he liked about money and stardom, but that was a front. Inside him there still lived a little boy, longing for his father's attention and the feeling that he belonged in the family that always seemed to exclude him. She tightened her arms, instinctively seeking to protect that little boy.

'Don't worry,' she said. 'I'm here as long as you need me.'

'Charlie—'

The doorbell rang.

'That'll be Rick, come to collect us,' Travis said reluctantly.

She raised a clenched first. 'Forward into battle.'

He mimicked the gesture. 'Victory awaits.'

They were to travel in an open car, the better to be seen. When they were seated in the back, Rick drove them down to where Joe was waiting with several of the others.

'Most of them have gone on ahead,' he told them. 'It looks more natural if we don't all arrive together. Let's get started.' But when he saw Travis's arm about Charlene's shoulders he looked doubtful. 'I'm not sure that's enough. Maybe you should be leaning close so that your head is resting on Travis's shoulder.'

'Occasionally,' Charlene agreed. 'But this journey is new to me, so I think he'd be pointing things out. I'd say, "Oh how wonderful!" and we'd interact.'

'Great! You've got a real talent for giving directions.'

'You're telling me,' Travis said with feeling. 'You should see how hen-pecked I am at home.'

Everybody laughed and they set off down the Santa Monica Freeway. It was a merry start to the day.

After an hour's drive they reached the roads that

led to the beach, and the car slowed down so that passers-by could see them. Now Charlene rested her head on his shoulder, as per instructions, and he laid his own head against her hair. Joe, overtaking, gave a thumbs up sign. Perfect!

About twenty of the crowd from the show had arrived before them and had taken over a small section of the beach, entertaining photographers with their antics while everyone awaited the star.

Vera, who'd looked after Charlene on the first day, approached, saying, 'Your changing huts are over here.'

They each vanished into a hut, emerging a few moments later to stand in the sun, breathing in the fresh air with expressions of ecstasy, while secretly sizing each other up.

Now Charlene knew she'd been right to come on this trip. Not for anything would she have missed the sight of Travis in tight black swimming trunks, reminiscent of the other night. He was everything she remembered, lightly tanned, smooth chested, the perfect combination of lean and muscular.

But he seemed less pleased, frowning a little at her modest one piece. 'I thought you'd have chosen a bikini.'

'Tut, tut!' she murmured. 'Your respectable girl-friend doesn't flaunt herself like that. Besides,' she added in a tone of coming down to earth, 'I'm too skinny for a bikini.'

'You're not skinny,' he said. 'Just beautifully slim. There are models who'd give their eye-teeth for your figure.'

'Thank you, kind sir, but I'd still like to be more curvaceous where it matters. Like here.' She wriggled her behind to give him a better view. 'Wouldn't that bit be improved by a little more oomph?'

'No,' he said with feeling. 'It wouldn't.'

'Oh, come on, take a proper look.'

'I am taking a proper look,' he said in a strained voice. 'It's perfect as it is.'

'Well, that's very kind but I suppose you've got to say it, haven't you? We both know I need a bit more there. Perhaps I should try to put on some weight.'

'I warn you, do that and you'll be sorry.'

'Ooh, the dominant male,' she teased. 'I thought you didn't do macho.'

'Maybe it's time I tried.'

By now they had reached the water. She hopped

in front of him, dancing backwards through the tiny waves.

'C'mon,' she taunted. 'Make me sorry.'

'Whatever could I do that would make you sorry?'

The thought, *You could send me away from you, and I'd be sorry for ever* flashed through her mind, but was banished. Nothing was going to spoil today.

'You'll never find out,' she said, moving faster.

But that was a mistake. She lost her balance and rocked wildly until he seized her and drew her against himself to steady her. She had a wild sensation of his bare chest against her and clung to him, wishing the rest of the world would just vanish.

Joe appeared beside them.

'Nice stuff, but go back to shore. Charlene, I don't want you swimming just yet because of your hair. Travis, why don't you carry her?'

'Happy to oblige,' he said, grinning and sweeping her up into his arms.

True to her role, she clung to him, shaking her head so that her hair could float in the sun. As they emerged from the water the rest of the cast was there, playing games, tossing balls about, cheering them.

Then Travis saw something that soured his mood.

'What the devil is he doing here?'

'Who?'

'Him.' He jerked his head in the direction of a young man capering by the water's edge.

'Oh, it's Lee,' Charlene said. 'Well, nearly everyone's here, so I suppose he was bound to be included. And look, there's Penny.'

Penny was laying firm claim to her fiancé, which should have eased Travis's mind, but didn't.

How did she feel about him? Travis wondered. She said it was over but now he knew that she was an accomplished actress. That was fine for presenting a mask to others, but he hated to think that she might be presenting a mask to him.

'Shouldn't you put me down now?' she said.

'Not until I have Joe's permission,' he said firmly, marching away up the beach.

She chuckled and buried her face in his shoulder. He only wished he could be sure she wasn't looking back at Lee.

Vera was waiting with a large white towel spread

out on the sand. Travis dropped to his knees and laid her out so that she showed to best advantage. Then he lay down beside her, propping his head up on one hand and gazing down adoringly.

She gazed back up, trying to match his expression. It was easy. Too easy, she thought with a flicker of alarm.

He's only acting, said the warning voice in her mind. *Don't forget that.*

And I'm acting too, replied her sensible self. *I'm not falling in love with him. I'm not! I'm not! I'm not.*

'Let's do this later,' she said. 'It's too soon to lie down.' She rose hurriedly, needing to get further away from Travis. This was dangerous.

Someone had brought beach balls, which were tossed high in the air. Much chasing and jumping followed, showing off several figures to advantage. But none were quite as fine as Travis's figure, Charlene thought with appreciation.

Following the 'stage directions', they held hands to walk along the water's edge, chased each other, laughed into each other's faces and generally gave an expert performance.

His arm about her was strong and delightful and

she was emboldened to raise her hand and lay it against his chest. She could feel the faint beat of his heart against her fingers and knew there had never been a moment as sweet as this in her life. Perhaps there never would be again, so she would remember and treasure this for ever.

'How are you managing?' he asked, leaning down so that he could speak quietly.

'I'm enjoying it. I said I'd do anything and I meant it.'

For a moment something flickered in his eyes. 'Anything at all?'

'What do you think?'

'I wish I knew what to think.'

From nearby, Joe, always keeping watch, complained, 'You both look too serious. Say something to each other.'

'You're treading on my foot,' Charlene told Travis fervently.

'Something nice,' Joe corrected.

'You're the most handsome man in the world,' she declared.

'Now you're just making him laugh,' Joe protested.

'What do you expect?' Travis demanded, grinning. 'How can anyone keep a straight face like this?'

Some journalists and photographers appeared.

'Hey, Travis, tell us about your lady. All Los Angeles is talking about her.'

'Then you don't need me to tell you,' he said in a voice that sounded slightly uneasy.

She wondered if he feared to offend her by saying too much and was sure of it when he patted her hand, murmuring, 'Don't worry.'

'Aw, c'mon. Just a quote. How did you meet?'

'We bumped into each other in the studio,' she said. 'I'd lost my way and he…he found it for me.' She gave a mysterious smile. 'Maybe. Now, I think that's all, don't you?'

As they resumed their walk she said, 'I hope you don't think I said too much.'

'That was brilliant!' Joe spluttered. 'The perfect story. You're really good at this, isn't she, Travis?'

'Yes,' he said quietly. 'She is.' He glanced over his shoulder at the paparazzi still in pursuit and said in a harassed voice, 'Don't they ever give up?'

'They're waiting for you to kiss her,' Joe informed him. 'Get on with it.'

He slid quickly away lest he be caught in the picture.

'He's right,' Travis said.

'Of course he is.'

'I'm sorry.'

'We have to be professional,' she assured him.

The sun was beginning to set, throwing a golden glow over the sand and making the water glitter. As if united by the same thought, they strolled a little way into the sea and paused, gazing into each other's faces.

Gently he pushed the hair back from her face.

'Time to be professional,' he said, and lowered his mouth.

She'd thought herself braced against the impact but knew instantly that nothing could have guarded her from the feel of his lips. Gentle, hesitant, then firm, pleading, enticing, commanding.

It was all an act, she reminded herself wildly—mostly on the surface to fool the cameramen, and just a little between them to provoke her into the right reaction. Nothing for real.

Remember that!

But it was hard to remember while she was held

so strongly against his chest, his bare legs against hers, his arm behind her head, holding her close.

Feelings chased each other through her in confusing whirls. Pleasure, excitement, a feeling that life had opened up new possibilities. But also fear, because she knew she was on the verge of losing control. She wanted him more—and more—and any moment now—

'That's it, gentlemen,' came Joe's voice out of the mists. 'Mr Falcon just wanted a pleasant day, without you invading his privacy. Time you went.'

Nobody was fooled but they had what they wanted, and they began to drift away.

'Are you all right?' Travis asked softly.

'Yes, I…I'm all right.'

'I'm sorry about this. It's not what you signed up for.'

'Everything's fine. I'm not going to make trouble, I promise you. Sensible and level headed. That's what we agreed, and that's what I'm giving you.'

He hesitated a moment, as though something had taken him by surprise. But then he gently released her, saying, 'Of course. I know you always keep your word. It's time we were going home.'

Now they would be alone and something more

might happen between them, she thought happily. But Joe intervened like an awkward demon, announcing that he'd booked a table for them at one of the city's most glamorous restaurants.

So the performance continued that evening under glittering chandeliers. They talked but it meant nothing. Charlene had a sense that he was keeping slightly distant, as though wary after the day's events. She could be patient. Perhaps when they got home he would speak more freely.

But at last he closed his eyes and said, 'I think I've had too much to drink. We should get home before I have an embarrassing collapse.'

He left with his arm around her shoulders, murmuring, 'You don't mind propping me up, do you?'

She patted his hand. 'It's what I'm here for,' she said tenderly.

Charlene looked forward to taking him home, seeing him warm and comfortable, even perhaps happy. That was really all she asked. That he should be happy.

There was no hint then of what was to come, and how it would devastate him.

CHAPTER TEN

AS SOON as they reached home Travis put on the television, as he always did, to catch up with the news. Almost at once he tensed, staring at the screen.

'Isn't that—?' Charlene gasped.

'That's my father,' he confirmed, turning up the sound.

'...people who remember Amos Falcon from the old days are intrigued to see him in action again, and this conference in New York...'

Dazed, Travis sat down on the sofa, his eyes fixed on the screen. Charlene sat beside him, trying to imagine how this would be affecting him.

It seemed that Amos Falcon had been in New York for three days, during which time he had attended meetings and socialised with men as wealthy as himself. The only thing he hadn't done was contact his son in Los Angeles.

Suddenly she felt Travis grow even more tense. Another man had appeared on the screen. He was in his thirties, had a facial resemblance to Amos and seemed on the best of terms with him.

'...his son, Darius Falcon, who once seemed to have withdrawn from the world of finance, but who'll be joining his father in this new opportunity...'

The item ended. Travis sat frozen.

'He's in New York,' he murmured. 'What time is it there?'

'Three hours ahead of us,' Charlene said. 'He should be in bed by now.'

'A good time to call him, then. No, wait.'

He began clicking buttons on his cellphone, looking for a message, Charlene thought. But there was nothing.

'They didn't say where he was staying,' she said. 'So where could you call him? Perhaps someone in his home would know. If you called—'

'No!' Travis interrupted her violently. 'Never.'

Of course he wasn't going to advertise that his father had ignored him, Charlene thought, blaming herself for thoughtlessness.

Travis named a hotel. 'He's always stayed there in the past.'

He dialled a number. Charlene moved quietly away. She had a horrible fear of what was about to happen, and knew he would hate anyone to see it.

But she left her bedroom door open and heard him say, 'Fine, when he comes in would you give him a message? I'll give you my home number and my cellphone. Any time will do, night or day.'

He hung up and turned to see her standing in the door.

'Goodnight,' he said. 'You've had a long, tiring day.'

His message was plain. He'd spoken often of their closeness and his reliance on her, yet she could not help him now.

Quietly she closed the door.

Twice more during the night she rose and looked out discreetly. He was still there, silent and motionless. Never once did the phone ring.

There could be a simple answer. Amos might have stayed out overnight, or returned late and noted the message for later. The call would come. Surely it must.

Over breakfast she asked for the latest news, not revealing how much she knew.

'I fell asleep,' Travis said indifferently. 'If the phone rang I might not have heard it.'

Her heart was heavy as she saw him off to work. Instinct warned her to fear the worst. She knew of Travis's feeling of isolation, of being shut out from the heart of the family. He was obsessively aware of his father's indifference to him, bordering on contempt. Now she saw the reality.

Amos had come to the country where his son lived but hadn't contacted him, or even told him in advance. When Travis reached out he'd made no response. And Travis had been forced to watch him with brother Darius, the favoured son, as he himself would never be.

But Amos would call. He must. He would probably use the cellphone and contact Travis at the studio. But just in case he dialled the landline she would stay in all day.

Hours went past in silence. In the early afternoon the phone rang and she seized it up.

'It's me,' said Travis's voice. 'Have there been any phone calls?'

'No.'

'I see. All right. I'll see you tonight.'

He came home early, questioned her with a look, and shrugged when she shook her head. He settled on the sofa, watching television news, seeking further information about Amos. But there was nothing.

She brought him some coffee. 'You look tired—'

The phone rang.

Their eyes met, sharing the same brilliant hope. He grabbed the phone.

'Hello? *Father!* Good to hear from you. I heard you were over here. Maybe we could meet. I can get a couple of days off to fly to New York—what's that? Oh, I see. Well, in that case—'

Curse Amos Falcon, she thought wildly. Curse him for daring to hurt Travis.

It broke her heart to see Travis's face as hope died from it, leaving behind a dismal nothing.

The phone call ended. He stayed sitting on the sofa as though too weary ever to move again.

'What happened?' she asked, going to sit beside him.

'He's on his way back to Monte Carlo,' Travis said in a blank voice. 'He called me from the airport.'

'Damn him!'

He shrugged. 'I mean nothing to him. Why should he pretend otherwise? Right, that's it. Time to be realistic. I think I'll go out. Don't wait up!'

'Can't I come with you?'

'No, it won't be the sort of evening that you'd enjoy.'

'Hey, stop there! Be careful. If you end up in a nightclub with a floozie it'll do you more damage than you could cope with.'

'No women, I promise, just—'

'Just too much to drink, huh?'

'Maybe just a little.'

She had a vision of the evening ahead if she left him unprotected. It wouldn't be like last night when he'd got faintly tipsy before going quietly home with her. This time there would be a little indulgence, then a lot, more and more. The word would go around, people would text and his enemies would be alerted. Suddenly everyone who wanted to damage him would converge.

'No way,' she said, taking hold of him. 'Don't even think of leaving.'

But he eased away from her.

'I'm going,' he said. 'I know you mean it kindly, but I can't shelter behind you for ever.'

'Travis, don't do this. It's dangerous.'

'That's for me to say. A man's entitled to behave badly sometimes.'

'Sure he is. And you behave as badly as you want, but do it here, with me. No witnesses. And if anyone asks if you behaved badly I'll lie my head off.'

'But that's just another way of sheltering behind you. Don't try to control me, Charlene.'

In despair she stayed where she was on the sofa, leaning forward with her head in her hands. This was what it had come to. She couldn't really help him at all.

'Come on, don't make so much of it,' he said, sitting beside her. 'I won't be long, but maybe it's time I let go of your apron strings. Hey, are you crying?'

'No,' she said huskily.

'Yes, you are. It'll be all right, I promise.'

She looked at him, defenceless, tears pouring

down her cheeks. 'Please,' she choked. 'Please don't do this. They'll be waiting for you. They always are.'

'Don't you think that sounds a bit paranoid?'

'Yes. I am paranoid. Sometimes paranoid is the right thing to be. Please, Travis, don't go. I'm not trying to control you. I'm trying to stop you losing everything.'

'I won't—'

'You will, you will. Oh, goodness, how can you throw it all away? Please—*please*—'

She was swamped by a sense of helplessness. His father's behaviour had had an unnerving effect on Travis, seeming to imbue him with a sense of self-destruction, so that only rebellion would calm his spirit. He would pay a heavy price for it, and she, who'd vowed to protect him, could do nothing. Her weeping became more desperate.

'Don't cry,' he said, brushing his fingers against her cheek. 'Please, Charlene, don't cry. I can't bear it. Look…look I—' There was a long silence.

She looked up, her eyes meeting his as she raised a tentative hand to touch his face.

'Don't go,' she whispered. 'Please don't go.'

'Charlene, what—?'

'Don't go.'

Now her fingertips were touching his mouth, drifting back and forth so that tremors went through him. Suddenly he seized her hand, kissing the palm fiercely, looking up with a question in his eyes.

'Please,' she murmured.

He gave a sudden groan. 'All right, I give in. I'll do whatever you want. You're the boss lady.'

She looked at him, unable to believe it. The feelings that had risen and swamped her made the tears flow more than ever.

'Don't,' he begged. 'Don't… Look…come here.'

His arms tightened about her, his lips brushed her wet cheeks.

'It's all right,' he said fiercely, '*it's all right*. I'll do anything you want. Just tell me and I'll do it.'

'I just want you to be safe,' she whispered.

'And I will be safe, as long as I have you.'

'You'll always have me.'

'Look at me,' he murmured, lifting her chin with his fingers.

There was a dark light in his eyes, not the anger that had been there before, but one that seemed to open a new door. If only she knew—

Their mouths were close and she could feel the warmth of his breath against her lips. Scarcely knowing what she did, she moved until they brushed softly against each other. It was the faintest touch, yet it was enough to bring back the moment on the beach when he had kissed her. She was shaking now as she had been then, and so was he. Now she sensed in him the same mixture of reactions—joy, disbelief, wonder, confusion—as she sensed in herself.

He lowered his mouth to touch hers more completely. Even then he was hesitant, but only for a moment, until he read the message of tender willingness in her lips, her hands touching his face. The wild excitement that had taken them by storm on the beach was there, but still lurking in the shadows, tempting them on with the promise of sweet discoveries, when they should have the courage to make them.

'Charlene—' He drew back a fraction. 'Do you think—?'

'Hush. What I think is…that this is no time for thinking.'

He hesitated only a moment, as if needing to be quite sure. Then he rose slowly, taking her hand for the short journey to his room. The huge windows, looking down over the lights of the city, were uncovered. But they didn't draw the curtains across. There was no need. Up here, in the dark, nobody could see them as their clothes fell away.

For a while, lying on the bed, they were strangely still, silently asking each other questions, seeking answers, happy when they found them. Then the first movements, tentative, discovering each other, realising that all was well.

His touch was gentle, fingers drifting across her naked skin, pausing, exploring slowly as though ready to retreat, but never doing so. She was glad of that. If he had stopped now she would have been devastated. She tried to convey her feelings through her own fingertips, caressing him softly, letting him know that this was right, perfect. The moment when she became his was the sweetest of her life.

Afterwards there was peace, the joyous satisfaction of lying back with his head on her chest, both of them totally still. In a few moments she was asleep.

She awoke in the early hours to find Travis restless, moving here and there as though desperately seeking something. His eyes were closed and his breathing deep. He still slept, but even in the depths of sleep something was disturbing him.

She touched him gently and at once he grew still. After a moment he moved again, reaching out until his hands encountered her, touched her face, her eyes, her lips.

'I'm here,' she whispered. 'I'm here beside you.'

Slowly she felt the tension drain from him. A long sigh came softly from his lips. He turned so that his head was resting on her shoulder, and after that he never moved again until they awoke together in the early morning.

He rested on his elbows to look down at her.

'Is everything all right?' he asked.

'Everything's fine with me. Did you have a good night's sleep?'

'I did in the end. I don't know what happened. I was restless for a while. I wanted to wake up but I couldn't make it happen. But then suddenly all the trouble vanished and everything was peaceful.'

'Dreams can be like that,' she whispered.

He stroked her face. 'Was it just a dream? Charlene, I don't know how to say this, but—'

'Then don't say it,' she whispered, her finger over his lips. 'Not now.'

He rose from the bed, divided by two conflicting desires, to be close to her, feeling her warmth and comfort enfold him again, and to be alone with his confused thoughts.

Which of them, he wondered, had led the other into the bedroom? He'd been the first to rise to his feet, take her hand and draw her after him. But he knew he would never have done so if he hadn't felt her willingness, sensed that she was urging him to take action and would be disappointed if he didn't.

So who had led who?

But there was another question, more urgent, more worrying.

Last night she had rescued him, as so often before. But who was the woman who had come into his bed? Charlene, the lover who had touched his heart? Or Charlie, the sister and protector who pandered to his needs like a nursemaid?

And if it was the second, might there not be a tiny hint of contempt in her kindness?

That thought made him shiver.

Over the next few days Charlene had the feeling that Travis had changed towards her. He never spoke of the passion they had shared, nor did his manner invite her to speak of it. He seemed uneasy in her company, as though he felt they'd come too close and was trying to step back. Several times he took her out to dinner, but always with other friends present. It was as though he didn't want to be alone with her.

She waited, hoping that he would open his arms to her and take her again into his bed, where they could rediscover the tenderness that had been so special. Then she would know what it had really meant.

But she waited in vain. Travis seemed to have put their lovemaking behind them as completely as if it had never happened. Sometimes she would look up to find him regarding her with a strange questioning expression. But when he saw her glance he would immediately begin to talk about something unimportant.

With pain and dismay, she realised that he'd turned to her, not in love but in need. She could give him something he'd found nowhere else, but he wasn't ready for the next step. Perhaps he never would be.

But she refused to give up hope yet. It would take

time for them to find each other, but she would be patient. There was everything to gain.

A location shoot caused him to be away in Washington for several nights. His calls home were cheerful, but left her wondering if he was glad to be away from her. Perhaps she would know everything when she saw him again.

But when she met him and Joe at the airport there had been a development that briefly blotted out everything else.

'I've had a call from Marcel,' he said. 'His wedding is next week.'

'Next week?'

'Yes, it's got to be fitted in with some money-making project.'

'How does the bride feel about that?'

Travis grinned. 'I should have mentioned; it's her money-making project. So next week we're off to Paris.'

'Can you get time off?' she asked.

Travis looked over his shoulder to Joe, walking just behind them. 'You said there'd be no problem, didn't you?'

'Sure thing,' announced Joe. 'Great PR stuff. You're a Falcon among Falcons. Big names. Lots of spotlight. Go to Paris, have a great time and do your stuff, both of you.'

The next few days were hectic. Travis devoted himself to filming while Charlene went on a shopping binge, accompanied by Julia, whose advice was expert.

She remembered their first evening in Los Angeles, discussing Shakespeare and the time she'd played the role of Helena.

Another unwanted female, she thought. *She spends most of the play trailing after her lover, begging him not to reject her. He comes back to her in the end, but only because someone has cast a magic spell on him. That's not the same as the real thing. Strange how I always got that sort of part.*

But was it really strange? she wondered. The plain one. The girl chosen as a last resort. The one with whom the hero would 'make do'. That had been her on the stage, and was it now, perhaps, coming true in her life?

Travis might one day come to love her a little, but not as she loved him. If there was one thing certain in the universe, it was that. He might make do with her. Children, stability, the feeling of being wanted for himself and not for his fame. These things were what he yearned for, and to win them he could decide to do without romantic love.

One of Helena's lines came back to her.

Love looks not with the eyes but with the mind.

Travis's eyes must have told him that she was plain, despite his kind remarks about her figure. His mind had told him that she had qualities of sympathy and understanding that he needed. But could that substitute for love?

Her own love had looked not with eyes that could be distracted by his handsome appearance, but with a mind and heart that saw the man who concealed himself from others, yet reached out to her. There was no way she could not have loved him.

On the day of departure he did a final session at the studio and she went with him, to be ready as soon as he'd finished. While he worked, Joe took her to the canteen. The two of them got on well, and he missed no chance to express his admiration for the service she was doing the studio.

'Thank heavens for you,' he said now. 'You're going to help him get that film part. The only reason Alaric Lanley is in the running is because he's better known. You help to keep Travis in the headlines, and that's good.

'This wedding is another chance. The Falcon dynasty, the great Amos—well, OK, maybe not great. People say he's the biggest bastard in creation, so how did he father a lovely guy like Travis? When you meet him, sweet-talk him, OK? Try to get a picture of the three of you together.'

There was serious doubt whether Amos would be there, but Charlene judged it more tactful not to mention this and slipped hastily away to powder her nose.

Returning a few minutes later, she could see that Joe was on the phone and was about to retreat when she heard him say, 'Look, Travis, why don't you just marry the girl? All right, all right, no need to blast my ear off—yes, I know but—Travis, will you listen to me? Charlene's good for you. I can see how well you get on and she'll keep you safe—there's no need to say that—I didn't mean to offend you. We'll say no more.'

Now she backed away hastily. She desperately needed to be alone to come to terms with the devastating conversation.

She hadn't heard Travis's end, but she didn't need

to. At the thought of marrying her he'd exploded. The mere idea of it offended him. Joe had spoken of safety and 'getting on well'. He was promoting a convenient marriage, and clearly Travis wanted none of it.

How ridiculous her dreams appeared now! All the signs had been there when they'd swapped jokes about their unromantic friendship.

'You're safe with me,' she'd said. 'You're not my type.'

He'd pretended to be insulted, but actually he was relieved.

Marry her? How he must be laughing at the thought!

When she was finally calm enough to return, she found the call finished and Joe cheerful.

'Travis called to say work's finished and we need to get over there fast. He's all ready to go and the photographers are in place.'

'Oh...yes,' she said uneasily.

'What's the matter? Why do you suddenly look like that? Not getting cold feet, are you?'

'No, of course not.'

'Too late for that. Travis needs you.'

'I'm ready,' she said at once.

She couldn't back out now without explaining why, and there was no way she could reveal what she'd just learned.

So she became an actress again, smiling for the camera, smiling for Travis, embracing him, letting him usher her into the car, waving to the little crowd that had gathered.

'I really need this!' he exclaimed, squeezing her hand. 'Time off in Paris, and you all to myself.'

'You're always with me,' she said lightly. 'You need to be with your family while you have the chance.'

'The family, yes.' His sudden beaming look touched her heart. 'As many of them as we can get together. Maybe all of them, I don't know—'

She gave a theatrically blissful sigh. 'Oh, I'm looking forward to this trip. I've always wanted to see Paris. And look, I can go exploring on my own if you want to spend time with your brothers with no womenfolk around.'

He eyed her ironically. 'Nice try, but I'm keeping my eye on you at all times.'

Charlene shook her head. 'That's one thing you don't need to do and you know it. Now, wave at the crowd. They're calling to you.'

As always, he did as required, performing perfectly, while wondering exactly what she'd meant by 'and you know it'.

CHAPTER ELEVEN

THE flight from Los Angeles to Paris was thirteen hours. Charlene dozed as much as she could manage, sometimes awakening to find him holding her hand. After many hours had passed they found themselves over the Atlantic.

'Is anything more boring than flying?' she murmured.

'Not much,' he agreed. 'You just end up staring at clouds that go on endlessly.'

'At least we've got this to read,' she said, taking out the brochure of La Couronne, the magnificent hotel that was the heart of Marcel Falcon's empire, which was where they were to stay for the next few days. The gloriously coloured pictures showed a building that was several hundred years old, originally built as a palace, home of the nobility, whose portraits were also included.

'They were executed in the Revolution,' Travis said. 'The house changed hands a few times until

Marcel bought it and turned it into a hotel. Last year he bought up a London hotel with the idea of duplicating La Couronne as The Crown. That's how he met Mrs Henshaw, who turned out to be Cassie, a girl he'd been in love with eight years ago.'

'Eight years,' she marvelled. 'And they found each other again after so long?'

'It's incredible, isn't it? But I guess if love is real it can overcome time.'

'That's not all it had to overcome,' she reminded him. 'His clumsy proposal—without asking her first.'

Travis grinned. 'That'll teach him not to take any notice of me.'

'Anyway, they got it right in the end.'

'So much so that Marcel has created a wedding chapel in the hotel, something he always refused to do before.'

'What about your father? Will he be there?'

'It isn't settled. He's not pleased about this wedding either. He wants one of us to marry Freya, his stepdaughter, but she actually helped Cassie raise the money to buy into the business.'

'I thought you said she raised it modelling.'

'Some of it, yes. But Freya topped it up with a loan of money that Amos had given her to provide a dowry. He hoped she'd use it to entice Marcel. Instead, she used it to see him married to someone else. According to Marcel, Amos is still seething.'

'Did you never talk to him again after he called from the airport?'

'No. I might as well not exist as far as he's concerned. The last time I saw him was almost a year ago, in Monte Carlo, where he lives for tax reasons. He had a heart attack and we all went there to be with him, in case it was the last time.'

'But he recovered, and you had the chance to talk to him.'

'Yes,' Travis said wryly. 'The chief thing I remember is him grunting, "Don't give up. You can still do better."'

'I suppose that's a kind of encouragement.'

'He didn't want to encourage me. Quite the reverse. He wanted me to get a "serious job". He's not going to change now. I just hope he's there and we can meet cordially.'

They started the descent. She looked down with fascination as Paris came into view below them.

Whatever else happened, there were things about this trip that she was going to enjoy.

When they had reclaimed their bags Travis looked around. Suddenly his face lit up.

'Marcel!'

There at the barrier a tall man in his thirties was waving eagerly. Beside him was a truly beautiful young woman, whom Charlene recognised as the glamour model in the magazine.

Their meeting was joyful. Marcel thumped his brother's shoulders and was thumped in return before everyone calmed down for the introductions.

Charlene never forgot her first sight of Paris. It was a glorious day, with the city showing at its glamorous best as they made their way to La Couronne. From the outside, the hotel still looked like a palace. Inside, it presented a traditional appearance, but beneath the surface was every modern convenience.

A man with a faint resemblance to Marcel was waiting on the huge stone stairway that led up to the hotel entrance. This must be Darius, Charlene thought, watching him greet Travis.

'Let's leave the three of them to talk,' Cassie said. 'I'll show you to your suite.'

Of course they had put them together, Charlene realised. To have asked for separate rooms when they were known to be living together would have invited suspicion.

'You're all on the same floor,' Cassie explained. 'Darius and Harriet have rooms just along the corridor, Jackson's around the corner, then Leonid, and over here is for Amos and his wife, and Freya.'

'If they come,' Charlene said wryly.

'I'm crossing my fingers. It will make Marcel very sad if Amos snubs him.'

They were accommodated in a grandiose suite, dominated by a double bed so huge that the occupants could hardly be described as sleeping together. Cassie showed her out onto the balcony, from where they could see a cab drawing up to the entrance and a young woman descend.

'That's Freya,' Cassie said. 'And she's alone. Freya! Up here!'

But no Amos, Charlene thought with sinking heart. She knew a spurt of anger at the thought of Travis's disappointment.

I'm being absurd, she reproved herself. *It's Marcel who's being rejected, not Travis.*

But she knew that he would feel it the most.

Freya and Cassie greeted each other as old friends, reminding Charlene that Freya had helped raise the money for the hotel investment. She was a brisk, efficient young woman, attractive without being glamorous. She and Charlene took to each other at once.

'Why are you here alone?' Cassie asked. 'Aren't Amos and your mother coming?'

'I hope so. I left them arguing about it. Amos is still displeased with me for helping Marcel to marry you, but he doesn't rule my life, and so I told him.'

'Good for you,' Cassie said at once, adding wickedly to Charlene, 'You want to watch out. He'll be trying to marry Freya to Travis next.'

Freya winked. 'Don't worry. Travis doesn't interest me.'

'It wouldn't bother me if he did,' Charlene said, laughing. 'Be my guest. He's all yours.'

'Excuse me,' said a voice from the door. 'Did I hear that right?'

Travis was standing there, clearly enjoying the joke. Freya threw herself into his arms with a delighted cry.

'Trust you to come in at the wrong moment,' Cassie observed.

He gave a melodramatic sigh. 'Don't worry, I'm used to rejection. Freya, it's lovely to see you.'

There came a noise from the corridor outside. Cassie and Freya dashed out, crying, 'Leonid, Jackson!' followed by Travis.

Charlene followed more slowly and received a surprise at the sight of the two men. One she recognised as Jackson Falcon, whom she'd often seen on television, fronting nature programmes. The other man bore such a strong resemblance to Travis that it was startling. He had the same lean features, generous mouth and dark eyes. The difference lay in the atmosphere that clung to him. Travis's air was light-hearted and charming. Leonid Falcon carried a brooding melancholy that seemed to come from a darker world.

He greeted everyone with quiet courtesy, speaking in a heavily accented voice, but then seemed to stand back, watching with cautious eyes.

Now Marcel and Darius were there, revving up spirits for the evening ahead.

'We're going to have a great party,' Marcel announced. 'It's too long since we all saw each other, and we're going to make the most of it.'

A cheer went up. The fun had started.

The family dined together. Charlene got on especially well with Harriet, Darius's bride from the island of Herringdean.

'Everyone wants to meet you,' she said, plumping down beside her and offering a glass of wine. 'The girl who's won Travis's heart.'

Charlene made a laughing reply, but the words, *If only,* flitted through her brain.

'You know, of course, how Marcel nearly ruined his own chances when Darius and I got married,' Harriet added.

'By taking my cue from my daft brother,' Marcel put in, joining them.

'Don't blame me,' Travis protested, appearing behind him. 'It was the character, a virtuous, magical being, not me. Some people can't tell the difference.'

'Nonsense. I could tell the difference between you and a virtuous being without any trouble,' Marcel declared, and a cheer went up from the others.

This was what Travis had secretly yearned for all

his life, Charlene thought; the support and cheerful companionship of people who were linked to him by unbreakable ties. She felt a glow of pleasure in the happiness he must be feeling.

La Couronne prided itself on being international. English and American newspapers were on sale, and the guests could receive television channels in several languages. So it wasn't a surprise when a pile of papers on a low table turned out to contain a showbiz publication, sporting the headline *Who Will Be The Man From Heaven?*

'Why, that's my brother, of course,' Darius declared with mock indignation. 'Nobody else need apply.'

Amid laughter, he read out a highly coloured piece about the rivalry between Travis Falcon and Alaric Lanley, phrased to make it sound as though the two were at each other's throats.

'"Both great stars,"' Darius read, '"both poised to seize the next huge chance and brook no opposition, both ready to explode in the firmament. The entertainment world watches breathless as these two giants fight it out."'

Cheers, laughter. Then sudden silence. Everyone

looked up to see a man and woman standing in the doorway.

The man was in his seventies, tall, white-haired, with features that were stern and uncompromising. He stood looking around at the gathering, as though their silence was a tribute that he accepted as natural.

Amos Falcon.

'Good evening,' he said.

Charlene had seen his picture in newspapers, but in the flesh he was different, more vibrant, more—she fought for the words—more menacing.

It was easy to believe that he'd made enemies, fought them, crushed them, seldom been defeated. Formidable as a foe, perhaps formidable as a friend, certainly formidable as a father.

At the sight of Travis he nodded, speaking gruffly but cordially. 'Glad to see you. Wasn't sure you'd make the journey, such a distance.'

'You don't think I'd let Marcel tie the knot without being there to chuck things at him, do you?' Travis grinned.

Then Amos did something that took everyone by surprise. Laying a hand on his son's shoulder, he said, 'Just make sure your aim is good.'

The others looked at each other, startled. Amos had actually made a joke, and with his least favourite son. Whatever was the world coming to?

To cap it all, when he made his way to a seat it was Travis he urged to come with him.

'Haven't seen you in a long time, except on television, of course. Can't get away from you there.'

'Sorry if that bothers you,' Travis said, knowing Amos had never been a fan of his career.

But his father surprised him again.

'Doesn't bother me. Good to see you doing well. Show business is like anything else. If you climb high you become somebody. There's profit to be had.'

'I think I'm beginning to understand this,' Harriet murmured. 'Somebody's told Poppa Falcon that Travis's career prospects have suddenly leapt up to the heights.'

'Right,' Cassie agreed. 'It's one thing to have a TV series, but quite another to be a big film star.'

'But does he know anything about film stars?' Charlene asked. 'I wouldn't think he acknowledged their existence.'

'I think I may be responsible for that,' Freya said

with a laugh. 'I've always been a big fan of Alaric Lanley.'

'I'm not surprised. He's gorgeous.' Harriet sighed.

Darius glanced up. 'Did you say something?'

'Not a thing,' she told him cheekily. 'Never mind me. Go back to making money.'

'Yes, dear.'

For a moment his severe aspect faded and he exchanged a conspiratorial smile with his wife that revealed a hidden world beneath their conventional exteriors.

How lucky they are, Charlene thought. Would it ever be the same for herself and Travis? They exchanged many smiles, even spoke with affection, but there was still a barrier that they hadn't brought down.

'Amos saw me reading stuff about Lanley,' Freya continued, 'and he started looking through it. That's how he discovered how big he is, how much money he's making, how he can take his pick of the roles.'

'Ah, I see,' Harriet murmured. 'So when he discovered that Travis was challenging him and was expected to win, suddenly Travis looked different.'

'Someone he might actually be proud of,' Charlene added. 'Even boast about.'

'And who'd make an amount of money that even Amos would have to take seriously,' Cassie added.

The three women nodded solemnly.

At last Travis drew his father in Charlene's direction.

'Father, there's someone I'd like you to meet.'

Amos knew her at once, she realised. Clearly he'd been following the press reports and needed nobody to tell him who she was or what part she played in Travis's public persona. He looked her up and down, nodding in a satisfied way. After that he spared her few words. If she'd been concerned for herself she might have been offended, but she cared only how this affected Travis, so she said what was necessary and retreated to leave him with his father.

The other women did the same, drifting to the far end of the room for a final coffee before bed.

'They'll probably talk all night,' Harriet muttered. 'I need a good sleep to get ready for tomorrow, and I'm sure Cassie does.'

'What about poor Charlene?' Cassie said. 'She must be so jet-lagged after that long flight.'

Yet, far from being jet-lagged, she felt vibrantly alive. At this moment she badly wanted to be with Travis, but she knew he would probably be a long time. At least, she hoped so. The longer Amos kept him there the better.

They were joined by Janine, Amos's current wife and Freya's mother. Charlene liked her at once, especially when she gave a humorous account of how she'd persuaded her husband to attend the wedding.

'He snubbed Darius's wedding. If he'd snubbed this one too he'd have looked ridiculous. Amos couldn't bear that.'

'He can't snub them all just because they don't marry me.' Freya chuckled. 'He'll run out of sons to snub. Silly man.'

'Don't let him hear you say that,' her mother warned. 'He's very fond of you. That's why he wants you in the family. But there's only Jackson and Leonid left, so you'd better make a choice soon.'

Freya glanced over to the corner, where Jackson and Leonid could both be seen.

'Perhaps I've already made it,' she said mysteriously.

They began to drift away. Charlene gave Travis a wave, then flapped her hand, indicating for him to go back to his father. He smiled.

She was feeling good as she went up to their suite. There she had a shower, donned a nightdress and settled down to watch television. By mysterious luck one channel had just begun to show *The Man From Heaven* with French subtitles, which she enjoyed enormously.

'Something funny?' Travis asked, coming in a couple of hours later and finding her laughing.

'You,' she said, pointing at the screen. 'There's no getting away from you, is there?'

He grinned. 'My father said something like that, but he actually seemed to think it might be a good thing.'

'It's really going well, isn't it?'

'Well, he's listening to what I say, which makes a change.'

'I'm so happy for you.' She threw herself back on the bed. 'Oh, it was a great night, even before he came. A real family occasion!'

'You mean with my brothers sending me up something rotten?' he said, grinning.

'Yes, exactly. That's what families do, send each

other up rotten, but still be there for each other.' She was helping him undress and hanging up his clothes.

'Isn't it lovely that your father's here?' she remarked.

'It's good for Marcel that he didn't snub him,' Travis conceded slowly.

'And you?'

'And me, yes. But—' he dropped down beside her and gently brushed the hair back from her forehead '—right this minute—'

'You know I'm here if you need me.'

'I do need you. You know that. You point the way for me, and somehow it always turns out to be the right way. I'm only afraid—' he stopped uneasily '—I'm afraid you've got the wrong idea now.'

'How have I done that?'

'This suite. I should have asked you first but I didn't tell them to put us together, they just assumed. Everyone thinks…I'm sorry if I've put you in an awkward position.'

She had hoped for much from this night, but now she sensed that emotionally he was backing away again, reminding her how shocked he'd been at the suggestion of marriage. But she concealed her disappointment.

'How have you put me in an awkward position?' she demanded. 'Everyone knows we're living under the same roof in Los Angeles. This was bound to happen. Now stop talking like a Victorian parson and come to bed, because the jet lag has caught up with me and I'm about to zonk out.'

'Me too,' he said, getting in beside her. 'As long as you're not offended.'

'Go to sleep!'

Next morning they were up early to prepare for the wedding. All around them they could hear the family in the other suites and sometimes outside in the corridor, where Freya was having a lively argument with her mother.

'If you really want to please your father, the answer's simple,' Charlene said as lightly as she could manage. 'Just marry Freya.'

He was sitting on the bed. Now he put his head on one side, seeming to consider.

'Really?' he mused. 'I don't think so. The fact is—I'd rather marry you.'

She hoped he didn't hear the little gasp that burst

from her. She knew he didn't really want to marry her. She'd been prepared for rejection, polite excuses as to why their relationship could go no further. This sudden reversal sent a jolt through her like a burst of lightning, but she controlled herself, assumed a smile, then her most cheerful tone to say, 'I'm serious.'

'So am I,' he said.

'No, you're not. It's one of your daft jokes. I blame Jackson. The pair of you are like a couple of school kids.'

'Then obviously I need a good teacher to keep me in line. But I take it you don't fancy the job.'

'I don't think I'd be up to it. It would take more than me to keep you in line.'

'No, just you. You're the only one who's ever come close. Even Mom admits that.'

'Oh, she wants to hand over the job of being your mother, does she? Thus freeing her for a succession of toy boys.'

His smile almost made her heart turn over. 'Something like that.'

She could hardly breathe. Beneath the teasing atmosphere, something serious was happening.

'Well?' he murmured.

'Well…the fact is…I'm not sure I'm up to the job.'

'You mean you don't think you could put up with me?'

'Maybe yes, maybe no. I never rush big decisions.'

'Then take your time.' He kissed her cheek. 'We'll talk again later.'

He vanished into the shower, leaving her stunned, not only by him but by herself.

Why hadn't she leapt at his offer of marriage? She loved him deeply. She wanted nothing more than to be with him for the rest of her life.

But his own feelings fell short of hers. That was the fact that she must face. He'd asked her because he'd decided to take Joe's advice. His career was going well. His relationship with Amos was going well, and he wanted to consolidate everything by making a sensible marriage to a woman who could care for him as no other woman could.

The temptation was fierce. *Seize the chance. Make the best of it. What else does life offer?*

If possible, she would have dismissed her sensible side, but it hammered on her brain for admittance, reminding her how devastating was the decision she must make.

To marry him, knowing that her feelings were far greater than his, and his merely practical affection could never reach the heights of her passionate adoration. Or refuse him, walk away, knowing she had left this vulnerable man at the mercy of what life would do to him.

Nonsense! This is a grown man. He doesn't need you to protect him.

But he does.

OK, so he marries you and you give him the children he wants. He's grateful and affectionate, and for a while everything is lovely. But then he gets infatuated with some sexy little bimbo. Maybe he won't leave you, but will he be faithful to you?

I don't know.

Yes, you do. Admit it.

I don't know!

CHAPTER TWELVE

LIKE everything else in La Couronne, the wedding area was magnificent. Chandeliers hung from the ceiling, gilt decoration adorned the walls.

'It's glorious,' Harriet said to Charlene, 'but I still prefer the ceremony Darius and I had on the beach at Herringdean.'

'That sounds lovely,' Charlene agreed.

'It was lovely,' Travis said. 'Especially with the dog there. How is Phantom, Harry? I know everyone was afraid he wouldn't live much longer.'

'He's managing to hold on. Every day is precious.'

'I'm longing to see what Cassie looks like in her wedding dress,' Freya said. 'She's so beautiful that I could hate her if I didn't like her so much.'

The room was packed. Marcel had few friends but many business acquaintances who appreciated the invitation, and much the same could be said for Cassie.

At last Jackson and Leonid entered, then Amos and Janine. Amos looked proud and magnificent. Nobody, Charlene thought, would have dreamt that he'd come to this wedding against his will.

Now Marcel appeared, taking his place at the front, with Darius, his best man. At last everything was in place for the bride's arrival.

As Freya had predicted, she was astonishingly beautiful. Charlene knew a pang. It wasn't fair that one woman could be like that and another… She looked down disparagingly at herself.

Marcel turned to watch his bride approach, and Charlene drew a sharp breath at his expression. It was possessive, adoring and slightly incredulous, as though he couldn't quite understand how such good fortune was his. That was how a man ought to regard his bride, she thought. It was how Travis would never regard her.

The voice of common sense echoed in her mind.

Time to face facts. Yes, I know you hate the thought, but listen. He doesn't really love you. Not as you love him. And he's never going to, you know that, don't you?

I guess I do.

So be sensible. Get out now.

But that means abandoning him when he needs me.

That won't be your problem.

Loving Travis will always be my problem. I can either love him at a distance, wondering how he is. Or I can love him close up, doing everything I can to make him happy.

And being hurt yourself. Think about it.

The same look was on Marcel's face when he finally led his new wife back along the aisle, followed by applause from the congregation.

Then the photographs, a dozen different combinations of family members. In one, Amos stood with all five of his sons. This was followed by pictures of Amos with Darius and Marcel, then Jackson and Leonid.

'Wait,' Amos called. 'We haven't finished. Travis, get over here.'

And so it came about that Travis was the only one of Amos's sons to be photographed alone with him.

'Yes,' Charlene murmured happily. 'Yes, *yes, yes*.'

The reception was a riot of speeches and champagne. Watching the bride and groom, Charlene saw the same look she'd seen on Marcel's face earlier. Darius too looked the same whenever his eyes fell on Harriet.

Would he look at you like that, at your wedding? demanded the sensible voice.

Probably. He's a very good actor.

At last the guests began to leave. The goodbyes were said, and the rest of the evening became an extension of the family reunion. Cassie and Marcel were staying in Paris that night, leaving for their honeymoon next day, when the rest of the family departed. Travis, Charlene was glad to notice, was deep in conversation with Leonid, whose grim air had vanished in the pleasure of his brother's company. As she passed by, both men reached out to catch her hand and drew her to sit with them.

'I was saying how glad I am to meet my brother again,' Leonid said, 'and how sad that tomorrow we must say goodbye, and not know when next we meet.'

Charlene was inspired.

'But that's easy,' she said. 'The show filmed an episode in London, so why not an episode in Moscow?'

'That's brilliant!' Travis exclaimed.

'But you are going to do the film,' Leonid protested. 'Will you have time?'

'I haven't got the film yet, and even if I do there are TV episodes to shoot first. I'll talk to them about this as soon as we get back to LA.'

'And they will say yes because you are a very big man and they do as you wish,' Leonid said triumphantly. 'Just wait until you get to Moscow and I can boast that this is my brother.'

He seized Charlene's hand and kissed it.

'Thank you for your idea. You are a genius. Travis, your lady is a genius.'

'I know that,' he said, regarding her with fond gratitude.

'Come on, I only suggested it.' She laughed. 'If they do this it will be to please Travis.'

'True,' Leonid agreed. 'Travis is the great man. But a great man needs a great lady beside him all the time.'

'He certainly does,' Travis said firmly. 'Damn! Why does the phone have to ring now? Hello, Joe!...What's that?' Suddenly his face brightened. 'Are you sure? It's not a mistake? That's great. Yes, I'll make a note of the date. Next month. Right.'

'What is it?' she asked.

'It's the nominations for the TopGo Television Drama Awards. Joe's had some advance notice.'

'And you've got a nomination?' Darius demanded. The family were gathering around them.

'More than one, apparently. Joe, how many? *How many?*' He looked around frantically. 'Paper—paper—'

Jackson produced a scrap of paper. Leonid shoved a pen into Travis's hands. Now everyone was riveted as he began to scribble.

'That's four!' Marcel exclaimed, reading over his shoulder as Travis hung up. '*Four* nominations?'

'Let's see,' squeaked Harriet. Seizing the paper, she began to read aloud. '"Award for the best performance by a leading actor in a television series. Award for the best comedy performance by an actor in a television series."'

'It's a con,' Travis groaned. 'There was one episode that was played for laughs, so someone's been pulling strings to get me this nomination. It doesn't mean a thing.'

'Stop being modest,' Jackson ordered. 'It doesn't suit you. What else is there?'

'"Award for the best dramatic performance by

an actor in a television play,"' Harriet read. 'You do one-off plays as well?'

'I did one last year. Just one.'

'And "best contribution to an educational feature,"' Harriet read.

Travis's brothers roared with laughter. 'Education?' Darius echoed. 'You?'

'Very funny.' Travis grinned. 'I made an appearance in a couple of documentaries. I told you, it's a con. Somebody's fixed this.'

'Of course,' Marcel declared. 'Nobody could ever think you were "somebody" just because you've got more nominations than the rest.'

Everyone cheered and applauded, raising their glasses in salute, while Travis looked modestly embarrassed even through his laughter.

Amos took the paper from Harriet and studied it.

'It's a fix,' Travis repeated. 'Nobody gets as many as that unless someone's pulling strings.'

'Of course,' Amos agreed. 'Obviously this is about boosting you for the film part. You will win everything. Your incredible achievement will be in the papers, and the part will be yours. Excellent.'

'You think that's good?' Travis queried.

'If you want something to happen, you have to

arrange for it to happen,' Amos told him. 'Clearly you are supported by big, important people.'

It was clear that Travis had gone up in his estimation. In Amos Falcon's world this was how things were done.

'You mentioned a date next month,' Amos said.

Travis nodded. 'The award ceremony is on the fifteenth, in Los Angeles.'

'Splendid. I shall be there.'

'And me,' Marcel said at once. 'And Cassie.'

'And me,' Darius added. 'And Harriet.'

Jackson and Leonid joined in, and with dizzying speed it was set up. All Travis's family, even Amos, would be there for his great event. Both professionally and personally, this would be his night of glory.

On the way up to their suite he was incandescent, whooping, 'You did it! You did it!'

'No, you did it,' she protested.

'Don't argue with me. You did it. Come here!'

He pulled her hard against him, kissing her with a fierce eagerness that brought her own desire rioting to the surface, overwhelming her despite her good resolutions. Only the sound of the elevator doors opening brought them back to earth.

'Come on,' he said, heading for their suite.

Once inside, he held her face between his hands, smiling into her eyes.

'Leonid's right,' he said. 'I need you beside me, so now you definitely have to marry me.'

'But—'

'No buts. I won't take no for an answer. Say you'll marry me.'

'Travis—'

'Say yes. Say it.'

Overjoyed but bewildered, she searched his face, desperately trying to understand something that could never be understood.

'Say it!'

'Yes,' she whispered. 'Yes.'

'You mean it? You won't change your mind?'

'I mean it.'

'Prove it to me.'

No need to ask what he meant. Even as he spoke, he was drawing her down onto the bed, and she went eagerly.

In the days after their first loving they'd been wary of each other, making her wonder if it would ever happen again. Now she understood how terrible that would have been. Never to have touched him again, or feel him touch her, never again to know the sweet thrill of being close to him, then closer until finally they were each other's with a completeness that made her dizzy with delight.

He loved slowly, even hesitantly, as though the first loving had left him still in doubt. But that was his way, she thought, trying to think clearly through a haze of pleasure. It was hard for him to be truly confident, even now, but surely it was in her power to find the way for him. With her arms firmly around him she gave herself up to the sensations and emotions that were like a new world: the world they would find together.

When he was asleep she rose and went to sit by the window, watching his still form on the bed. Common sense was still raging at her, and she knew she must tell it to stop its nonsense once and for all.

You did it. You gave in, settled for second best.

Travis could never be second best.

But what he's offering you is second best, and you know it. Is it coincidence that it happened tonight? You proved your usefulness again with that Moscow suggestion, and now he's definitely not going to let you go.

I don't want him to let me go.

But what's he offering? Love?

I don't know.

Yes, you do. He's not in love with you, not the way you are with him.

But he needs me, and I'll be there for him. And if…if one day it's over, I'll still be glad of the time we had together.

This is the twenty-first century. What happened to liberated woman?

I guess I'm not very liberated where Travis is concerned. And that's fine by me. I'll love him and cherish him, and give him whatever I can. And if he's happy, that's all I ask. Now go away and don't come bothering me again.

Silence!

Back in Los Angeles, everything was humming as preparations were made for the big night. Rumours had gone around about what was to happen, and the announcement about the film that was expected afterwards. Everyone who was anyone was determined to be there.

One disappointment was that her grandparents couldn't make it. Their holiday would be over just two days before the award ceremony, and they would be too tired from the long flight home to embark on another to Los Angeles.

'Could they change the flight?' Travis suggested. 'Come straight here from Africa, then stay with us for a while to get their strength back before returning to London?'

But when Charlene suggested this to Frank on the phone, he thanked her but refused.

'Emma's worn out. She needs to get home. We'll watch it on television. You'll hear us cheering.'

'What a shame,' Travis said. 'It would have made everything perfect to have them there, especially when we tell everyone our news.'

He planned to cap the evening by announcing their engagement.

'I'd better do it when I receive the first award,' he mused, 'in case there aren't any others.'

'You know how many there are going to be,' she said. 'This is going to be your night.'

His night in every way. Two days before the event, his family began to arrive. Amos, Janine and Freya dined with them and Charlene was struck by the look of pride and satisfaction on Amos's face.

He's got what he wanted from his father at last,

she thought. *At least, he's nearly got it. Don't let anything happen to spoil it now.*

Her dress for the evening was a magnificent dark blue velvet with a tight waist and long flowing skirt. Travis helped her on with it, and zipped it up.

'I like that blue,' he said. 'It goes well with this.' He showed her a ring of diamonds and sapphires.

'Let me wear it now,' she begged.

'No, we agreed I'd give it to you when I make the announcement.' His eyes were teasing. 'Until then, you'll have to be patient.' He kissed her.

'I'll try. Oh, Travis, I hope tonight is everything you hoped for.'

'If you're there, it will be. Hell! What's that?'

'My phone. Hang on, I'll get rid of them quickly.'

'Charlie?' It was her grandfather's voice. 'Something terrible's happened.'

'What?' she asked, but she knew the answer before he spoke.

'Emma's had a heart attack, a big one. Oh, darling, they say she might not last the night.'

'Sweet heaven,' she whispered.

'Can you come? It could be for the last time. She said I wasn't to call you because you had this other thing happening but—'

'Of course you were right to call me,' she said, almost violently. 'I'll be on the next plane. Which hospital?'

She wrote it down and said, 'Tell her I'm coming. Tell her I love her.'

'Emma?' Travis asked as soon as she hung up. He'd been watching and listening, motionless.

'She's had a heart attack. She's dying.'

'Then we've got to get over there fast. There's a flight this afternoon.'

'We—? No, Travis, you can't come. You've got the awards ceremony and those people will be there—your family—'

He stared at her. 'Are you seriously saying that you think I'll put all that stuff first? Before you?'

'You must. You can't miss tonight when there's so much hanging on it. I know you'd come with me if you could, and I'll treasure that. But you *can't*. Surely you can see that you can't?'

'What I can see—' he said slowly '—is something I never saw before. I didn't understand—but I do now.'

'You know I'm right,' she said. 'This is your big moment. I won't let you lose it because of me.'

He moved away from her. 'You'd better get

ready while I make the arrangements,' he said. And walked out.

While she threw some things together in a small bag she concentrated fiercely on the task in hand. If she let her thoughts get out of control she feared she would break down. Travis had said the right things about wanting to come with her, but he'd let her talk him out of it more easily than she could have dreamed.

And that was how things were between them. She'd told herself that she was willing to settle for second best, but she hadn't expected the reality to become so brutally clear so soon.

She changed into sensible clothes, taking just enough to manage. When she emerged, Travis was sitting at the table hurriedly writing something.

'It's all settled,' he said, folding the paper into his pocket. 'I've called the airport and fixed your ticket. Rick will take us.'

'Us?'

'I'm just coming to see you off.'

He opened the door, ushering her out before she could protest. She was struck by how cool and businesslike his manner had become. This was a practical man who'd dealt with the emotion, brushed it aside and was ready to get on with the important things in life. She felt a chill run through her.

The car was waiting, with Rick at the wheel. Once inside, she dropped her head in her hands and sat motionless. Travis put his arms around her, drawing her close. She reached out slightly, trying to respond, but she felt abandoned in another world, one that he wasn't part of, no matter how much he pretended.

'We're nearly there,' he said.

She pulled herself together. In a few moments they would part. She would return to her world, he would return to his, and who could say if they would ever meet again? At this moment she doubted it.

Now the rest of her life stretched ahead, empty because she would lose him, but even emptier because he would no longer be the man she loved and believed in.

As he helped her out of the car he called to Rick, 'Wait for me in the car park. I won't be long.'

'Perhaps you should go back now,' Charlene said.

'No, I've got time to see you into the Departure Lounge. Sit over there while I collect your ticket.'

He returned a few minutes later, handing her the ticket.

'Luckily you've only got hand luggage,' he said. 'So we can go straight to Check In.'

Closer and closer, the final moment approached. At the Check In desk she showed her ticket, received a boarding card and turned to say goodbye. But Travis wasn't looking at her. He was leaning over the desk, showing another ticket, receiving a boarding card.

'Travis, what—?'

'You didn't really think I'd let you go alone, did you?' he said.

'But you can't— The awards—'

'They'll have to do them without me.'

Joy and horror warred in her: joy at his generosity, horror at his sacrifice, rendering her speechless. While she floundered he urged her forward, brooking no resistance, and by the time she could think clearly they were in the Departure Lounge.

'Travis, how did you—?'

'A little bit of stage management. When I booked your ticket I booked one for me as well. Then I called Rick, told him what I was doing. He'll be halfway back to town by now.'

'But you told him to—'

'To wait in the car park, yes. But he knew I didn't mean it. It was just to fool you, so that you wouldn't suspect until it was too late.'

'Travis, please, be sensible. The studio bosses will be furious—'

'Let them.'

'Your family—'

'I called Darius. He said I was doing the right thing and he's going to explain things to the others.'

'And your father?'

'I'll have to call him separately. In fact I'll do it now.'

But he was saved the effort by the ring of his phone. It was Amos, speaking in a voice so sharp and loud that Charlene could hear it from several inches away.

'Have you gone mad?' Amos raged.

'Father, I'm sorry to let everyone down like this, but I had no choice.'

'Of course you had a choice. You've risked everything you've worked for, you've insulted me. What kind of a fool do I look now, turning up to see you win prizes and you can't be bothered to be there?'

'I never meant to insult you. I hoped you'd understand.'

'I understand that you're doing something criminally stupid. That any son of mine—'

'Right this minute I don't feel like your son,' Travis interrupted him. 'And that makes me glad.'

'Stop talking like that and get back here at once. I'm telling you, no woman is worth it—'

His voice stopped suddenly. Travis had hung up.

'You cut him off,' Charlene said, aghast. 'He'll never forgive you.'

'And I will never forgive him for insulting you.'

'But listen—' she seized him '—it's wonderful of you to be prepared to do this for me, but you mustn't do it. Go back. It's not too late.'

'Haven't you understood yet? It was too late from the moment I met you. I didn't realise it then. It took me too long to see it, but now I know that you're the only woman I could ever love.

'I've never been able to speak of love before because I wasn't sure of you. First there was Lee. I thought you wanted him, but then you seemed to let him go easily, and I began to hope. But you see—' he made a helpless gesture '—I don't just love you. I need you. I depend on you. We've always made jokes about that but I began to be afraid in case you just saw me as some clinging juvenile. Suddenly it wasn't a joke any more.'

One day she would try to explain that she rejoiced in his need of her. Being needed was almost as beautiful as being loved. But there would be time for that later.

With shining eyes, she gazed at him.

'But think of all you might be giving up—'

'All I can think of is what I'll gain. If I'd let you go alone it would always be between us, that I wasn't there for you when you needed me. You'd have been nice about it, but we would always have known. And something would never have been right for us.'

'But do you really understand what you might be losing?'

'Yes, I know what I might lose. I might lose *you*. I might lose the woman I love more than anyone in the world. With you would go all my chance of happiness, of a future that meant anything. I'd lose my hope of children, for if you aren't my children's mother, nobody else ever will be. I'd lose all purpose in life. I'd lose everything.'

Now she was beyond speech, gazing at him, trying to understand the glimpse of his heart and soul he'd given her, and which was so unlike anything she'd imagined. She'd thought she understood Travis so well. Now she saw that she'd never understood the first thing about him.

'You didn't know I felt like that about you, did you?' he asked gently.

She shook her head. 'I thought the love was mostly on my side. I love you so much it scares me.'

'But you always kept so cool. Even when you agreed to marry me it was as though you were being cautious—'

'I was. I thought you only half wanted to. I heard Joe talking to you on the phone. He suggested that you should marry me, and you lost your temper at the other end.'

He groaned. 'Of course I lost my temper. I was mad at him for daring to think I'd marry you as a PR stunt. I loved you. I was trying every way I knew to win your love, and I felt he'd insulted you. That's why I got mad. And you thought—Oh, good grief!' He pulled her against him. 'How did we ever find each other when we've taken so many wrong turnings?'

'But we found the right road in the end,' she said.

'You thought I asked you to marry me as a career move? That's why you didn't want me to come to London with you?'

'I don't want you to risk losing everything.'

He shook his head. 'If I don't lose you, I haven't lost anything. If I do lose you, I've lost everything. Promise to stay with me, and that's all I ask.'

'I'll stay as long as you want me.'

He kissed her, and would have said more but for the loudspeaker. It was time to board.

They said little on the journey. Everything that mattered had already been said, and they sat resting against each other, sometimes dozing, sometimes basking in their mutual contentment and joy.

In London a cab took them to the hospital. As they arrived they exchanged a fearful glance. In a moment they would know—

Frank looked up as they entered the little ward.

'Thank goodness!' he said fervently. 'Emma, darling, look who's here!'

Her eyes were open, and even in her dreadfully weakened state she could recognise them.

'Charlene—I knew you'd come.'

'And look who I've brought to meet you,' she said.

'But he's— This is—'

'This is your future grandson-in-law,' Travis said. 'And now you've got to get well fast, because we want to see you in Los Angeles for our wedding.'

'Oh, darlings! How wonderful!'

'Don't get agitated,' the doctor warned.

'I'm not agitated. I'm happy. I'm going to be there.'

She closed her eyes, smiling.

They stayed in the hospital for the rest of the day and all night. Now and then Emma would awaken, always a little stronger than before.

'The doctor says her chances are improving by the minute,' Frank told them. 'It means the world to her that you gave up so much to come here. Thank you with all my heart. But were you wise to do it?'

'It was the wisest thing I ever did,' Travis said with a tender glance at Charlene.

They left the hospital that evening and spent the

night in a nearby hotel, ready to return if there was an emergency call. But no call came.

As they snuggled down in each other's arms Charlene's thoughts were far away in Los Angeles, where the crowds would be gathering for the award ceremony, and people would be exclaiming in surprise, and perhaps annoyance, because the star of the evening wasn't there. She wondered how Travis felt now that the moment had come. But when she looked at him his eyes were closed. He might almost have been asleep, except that he turned and pressed his lips against her forehead.

Was he regretting his decision? Would he tell her if he did?

At last she fell asleep. In the early hours she awoke to find him just hanging up the phone.

'Any news?' she asked tensely.

'Yes, I called Joe. The awards ceremony was a success. I won the dramatic actor in a series award.'

'Not the other three?'

'No, but one is enough for me. Joe said they told the audience where I'd gone and why, and they applauded. We'll start work again as soon as I return. So you see, I've suffered no harm.'

'What about the film part?'

'Well—'

'Oh, no!'

'That's gone to the other guy. But who cares? I still have the series. And I have you. There'll be other film parts. But there won't be another you. My darling, try to understand. I've made my choice and I won't regret it. At least, I won't regret it as long as you stay with me, and love me.'

'Do you doubt that?' she whispered.

There was a strange look in his eyes, a mixture of teasing and adoration.

'What is it?' she asked.

'I was thinking that if Joe was here, he'd want you to say something nice to me. You wouldn't like to do that, would you?'

She considered. 'I might. I could say that I love you, that I've never loved anyone in my life as I love you, and I know that I never will. You *are* my life. I can have no other, and I want no other. I'll stay with you for ever, loving only you. And when the end comes I hope we'll still be together.'

She reached up to touch his cheek. 'Do you think that will do?'

He smiled, taking her hand and brushing it with his lips.

'That will do perfectly,' he said.

* * * * *